I0673347

GROUNDED IN THE WIND

GROUNDED IN THE WIND

PARKS PAT MYSTERIES
BOOK THIRTEEN

P.D. WORKMAN

 PD WORKMAN

Copyright © 2025 by P.D. Workman
All rights reserved.

No part of this book may be reproduced in any form or by any electronic or mechanical means, including information storage and retrieval systems, without written permission from the author, except for the use of brief quotations in a book review.

ISBN: 9781774688434 (KDP Paperback)
ISBN: 9781774688441 (KDP Hardcover)
ISBN: 9781774688465 (Lulu Paperback)
ISBN: 9781774688458 (Large Print)
ISBN: 9781774688472 (Digital)
ISBN: 9781774688489 (Auto-narrated audiobook)

ALSO BY P.D. WORKMAN

FIND MORE BOOKS AT PDWORKMAN.COM

MYSTERY/SUSPENSE:

Gentle Angel

Rushin' Death

Posed for Death

Death of a Corpse

Endowed with Death

Shattered to Death

Captured in Death

Currying Death

Healed to Death

Death's Charm

Bleeding Hearts Valley Thrillers

An Abrupt Departure

High-Tech Crime Solvers Series

Virtually Harmless

Cowritten with D. D. VanDyke

California Corwin P. I. Mystery Series

The Girl in the Morgue

Stand Alone Suspense Novels

Looking Over Your Shoulder

Lion Within

Pursued by the Past

In the Tick of Time

Loose the Dogs

AND MORE AT PDWORKMAN.COM

For the heroes who don't wear capes
At least not in public

STYLE NOTE

Since my largest readership is in the USA, I have chosen to use US spellings throughout this series. That includes the Americanization of centre to center, even where it is an actual place name, just for consistency's sake. I apologize to my Canadian readers for this.

I have chosen, however, to use Canadian grammar, particularly for Canadian voices. If you see what you think is a grammar error, it may just be Canadian, eh?

CHAPTER ONE

he day began like any other. Things had been pretty quiet on the homicide front, so the team had been working other Major Crimes cases, reviewing some cold homicides for any old evidence that might benefit from modern technology—such as more sophisticated search techniques, cutting-edge DNA testing, or an appeal to the public through social media. Margie looked forward to going home and spending some time with Christina at the end of the day. Her teenage daughter was getting older and more independent, and they didn't get nearly as much time together as Margie would have liked. Between Margie's work, Christina's school schedule, and Tracy, Christina's "friend who was a boy," it could be hard to connect for any meaningful length of time.

Margie had reached out lately to her cousins, now that more public gatherings were allowed, and was trying to arrange some extended family activities to reconnect them with some of the tribal "brothers" and "sisters" she had lost touch with since she had been Christina's age. She wanted to keep Christina connected with the Métis community, something that had not been easy during the early COVID months when they had first moved from Winnipeg to Calgary.

But tonight, they were planning a movie marathon, just Margie and Christina, bingeing Batman movies. Margie honestly wasn't that excited about the newest Batman, but was looking forward to some of the cheesier early TV episodes and movies.

Staff Sergeant MacDonald came out of his office and whistled to get everyone's attention, something she had never seen him do before. The effect was, therefore, instant. Everyone froze. Any banter between the detectives ceased, fingers froze over keyboards, and everyone looked at the tall, gray-haired man to see what was happening.

"We've got an incident," MacDonald announced. "A possible attack directed at the airport. A drone has been launched and has disrupted flights. The airport is locked down, all flights in and out have been suspended until the drone can be neutralized. Police all over the city are being scrambled to deal with the threat to public safety and ensure that the public does not panic. Messaging is that the source and intent of the drone are unknown, but there is no apparent danger to the public."

"*Is* there a danger?" Cruz asked.

"If there was going to be a weapons attack, it would likely have been deployed by now. It may be that the pilot lost control of the drone, it is being directed by someone without any real training or understanding of the restrictions they operate under, or that it is an act of mischief."

"Are they going to shoot it down?"

"They have methods to deal with it. Our job is to check out a potential launch area and see if we can locate the point it went up from and the pilot."

Margie's heart was pumping hard and fast. Even though

it didn't sound like the drone was actually any threat, it was still very different from what they handled on a day-to-day basis and would unfold quickly. It was a dynamic situation that would require all of them to be at the top of their game to see that the public wasn't put at risk and didn't panic over nothing.

"Where are we going?" Kaitlyn Jones asked as everyone rose from their seats and quickly pulled on jackets, preparing to go.

"Prairie Winds Park is the apparent point of origin," MacDonald announced, "given the reported sightings."

Margie glanced around at the others, hoping they had a better idea of where Prairie Winds was than she did. She vaguely remembered it as a park the Calgary cousins had spoken of sledding at when they were all still kids. But Margie had rarely been to visit Calgary during the winter. When she had, they had found smaller hills close to home or gone skating at Bowness Park.

"I will send you all the GPS coordinates and you can use your maps apps if you are not familiar with it," MacDonald advised. "We will all be heading out at the same time and can probably travel as a convoy, but if you get separated we don't want anyone getting lost."

"You're going too?" Margie asked, surprised. MacDonald generally worked from the office and dealt with the mayor's office or other political situations rather than going to crime scenes.

"In this case, I think it is best that I be on site to deal with any communications issues immediately."

Margie nodded, as did the others, and they quickly prepared to leave. Margie's phone chirped, and she saw the GPS coordinates MacDonald had broadcast, underlined as a link that meant her phone recognized the data format and would open it in her maps app, as MacDonald had suggested.

"Do you want to go together?" Jones asked Margie.

Margie grimaced. Unfortunately, her poor sense of direction had become legendary in the department. Even with GPS directions, it would not be unusual for Margie to miss an exit or take a wrong turn and add an extra twenty minutes to the trip to a location that should have been easy to find. Margie was sure that neither the French explorers nor the Cree making up her Métis heritage would have been very impressed by her ability to navigate by map or by memory.

"What part of the city is it in?"

"Northeast. If you started at your house and went north up Fifty-Second—"

"Uh, right." Margie nodded. Considering the time and the fact that Jones would have to drive Margie back downtown to pick up her car after however long it took them to deal with the drone incident, Margie thought it was best not to impose on Jones. "I'd better take my car. Who knows how long this will take. We will probably be heading straight home afterward."

Jones nodded and pushed back a curled lock of blond hair that had escaped her bobby pins. "You're probably right. It shouldn't be too hard for you to get to, even if we get separated. We'll probably take Deerfoot, turn off at McKnight—"

"I'll just follow everyone else or the GPS," Margie interrupted. "There's no point in telling me the route ahead of time."

"You should just ride with someone else," Gagnon told her as he headed for the door. Though Margie noticed he did not offer to drive Margie as Jones had.

CHAPTER TWO

*W*ithin a few minutes, they were down to their cars and headed out in a convoy to the park.

No one had made any jokes about Detective "Parks Pat" being on this call. It was not her usual callout to a park because she had been specially requested by someone who thought she should be there to investigate a homicide in a park, since that was *her specialty*.

Not that Margie *had* any particular talent for solving murders that took place in parks. She couldn't track and was more likely to get lost than anyone else if she set off on a hiking trail alone.

She kept focused on Jones's car in front of her, following as closely as she could without putting herself in danger of rear-ending her at the speeds they were traveling. Deerfoot had a speed limit of 100 kilometers per hour, and escorted by patrol cars with flashing lights, they were quickly passing all other traffic. They would beat the 18 minutes predicted by her maps app.

Margie let her eyes stray to the sky once or twice, wondering whether she would be able to spot the drone or any military aircraft sent to take it down. Surely they wouldn't shoot it down over the city, even over an airport runway.

Would she even be able to see it? They hadn't been given any details on the size of the drone, whether it was a child's toy, the type that could deploy a missile, or something in between. She assumed it wasn't the missile type, if it had been launched from a park. But she couldn't imagine a child's toy causing a panic at the airport, either.

The other cars in the convoy were exiting, so Margie followed suit. At the speed they were driving, she probably would have missed the exit if she had been on her own. So much of the time, it seemed that her maps app did not inform her of an exit until she had passed it. It couldn't just be hers. Did everybody else experience the same thing, and they were just better at anticipating a turn or recovering from a wrong move? She didn't understand how she could be that much worse than anyone else when she was being directed by a computer. She also had the ability to make several wrong turns in a row trying to get back on track, while others recovered after the first one.

They had to slow down considerably to crawl through the curving, single-lane roads in a retail shopping area, so she figured she would be able to stay with the rest of the convoy without getting lost.

In a couple of minutes, they were pulling into the parking lot of Prairie Winds Park. They didn't take the time to find individual parking spots, but instead pulled onto the grass. Margie looked around. It didn't appear to be a large park. Not like Glenbow Ranch, Fish Creek, or Nose Hill. There was a splash park and some playground equipment. The big sledding hill was the central feature of the park, and Margie figured that was the most likely place to launch a drone. It had only a few trees at the top, with wide grass expanses encircling it. It was higher than anything else in the area. A good reason for the authorities to suspect this was where the drone had been launched from. MacDonald gave directions, sending his detectives around and up the hill from various directions. They would all converge at the top, having covered most of the park so they could report anything suspicious and work out a plan of action.

Margie and Detective Jones took the right-hand trail after walking through the playgrounds. They encouraged people to leave as they walked through, trying to make their warnings sound stern but not frightening enough to make people panic. "We are investigating a situation. We need people to return to their cars for their own safety. Please move along..."

More law enforcement officers would be arriving to help evacuate the park, so they didn't spend much precious time encouraging those who were resistant. They had a situation to investigate. Margie kept her eyes peeled for anything that might be a remote control for a drone, for any weapons, and for anyone who looked suspicious.

It wasn't the kind of situation where they could weed people out by whether they had children with them or not. There were plenty of people who went to the park alone, from athletes obviously training for their particular sports to seniors with walkers or hiking poles walking only the flat areas or the gentle slopes. Some children didn't seem to be attached to any of the adults present, but Margie figured that if anyone were to approach them and try to engage them or remove them, their parents would quickly make themselves known.

They walked along the pathway, heads on a swivel, checking 360 degrees around them for anything out of place or that might flag the launching point of the drone.

Margie had expected it to be pretty clear who was

involved. She had thought the culprit would be showing off, making a big deal of what he had done, even if he knew it was illegal. But there was no launchpad that she could iden- tify. No man or group of teens standing around a controller or staring up at the sky. Margie and Jones had worked small drones with cameras when they had been looking for evidence in Edworthy Park on a previous case, so she had some idea of what to look for.

"Have you seen anyone with a drone or controller?" they asked various people they encountered on the path, before directing them back to the parking lot.

"What is this?" demanded a dark-skinned man in a gray hoodie. "Where did you all come from, and what is this all about? I have a legitimate reason to be in the park; you can't just kick us out of a public place."

Margie looked him over. His racial origins weren't clear. He could be Hispanic or Indigenous, or a mix of any number of races. Was it possible he was Middle Eastern? Was it bad that her mind went there when they were investigating a potential terrorist act? His loose hoodie could be hiding weapons in his waistband or pockets. She didn't like the way he moved his hands as he talked or how confrontational he was.

"Sir, could I get you to put your hands on your head, please?" Margie instructed him in a steely cop voice, "Inter- lace your fingers."

"What?" he blustered, "You don't have any right to come around here and order me around. I'm not doing anything wrong, working out at a public park." He still gestured as he spoke.

"Hands on your head, now!" Jones ordered, her voice a shade louder than Margie's. They wanted to control him, but not cause concern or panic among the other park users. They didn't even know if he were anything to be concerned about at this point. They could be putting themselves at risk from another direction by focusing on an innocent bystander not accustomed to following orders.

The man's eyes widened and he tried to watch them both as they approached him from different directions, each with their hands on their service weapons.

"Whoa, whoa, whoa," he said defensively, bringing his hands up to ear level and no longer gesticulating. "No need to overreact, here."

"Hands interlaced behind your head," Margie told him.

CHAPTER THREE

The man in the hoodie finally complied, putting his hands on his head and interlacing his fingers. He still jiggled his body a little, nervous or high; it wasn't immediately apparent which.

"I'm going to lift your sweatshirt to check underneath," Margie told him. "Are you carrying any weapons?"

"No!"

"No firearms, nothing sharp? Knife? Needle?"

"No! Who do you think I am? I'm just here to do my workout. My training."

Margie made sure that Jones had the guy covered and stepped close enough to lift his sweatshirt to make sure he didn't have any guns in his waistband or pockets. She patted the hoodie pocket and the warm-up pants pockets and could feel nothing but his cell phone.

"What is your name?" she asked him.

"Jordan. Jordan Brown. I'm here to work out."

"Well, like we told you, Jordan, we're trying to conduct an investigation and to keep everyone safe. We need you to head back to the parking lot and go home. I'm sure you can pick up your training schedule again tomorrow. But today is a wash. You need to move on."

"I can put down my hands?"

"Yes, thank you for your cooperation."

"What's going on?"

"Watch the news tonight. I'm sure it will be public by then. For now, we can't tell you anything except that you need to leave the park."

He looked around, more nervous than confrontational now, but still jittering like he was high. "Is it a bomb threat?" he asked, voice pitching higher.

"No, sir. Please don't repeat that where other people will hear it. We don't want to start a panic."

"But it's something that could hurt a lot of people." He looked around. "What's going on?"

"How long have you been here this morning? Have you seen anything unusual?"

"I don't know, maybe half an hour. I haven't seen anything. Anything like what?"

Jones shrugged. "Just anything you don't normally see here," she contributed. "Do you work out here a lot?"

"A few times a week."

"You see a lot of the same people, doing the same things."

"Yeah."

"Nothing out of the ordinary today?"

He frowned and looked around. "It's mostly the regulars. There are always people I don't know, though."

"Okay, go back to your car, please."

They saw him on his way and kept going along the trail, picking up the pace a bit since they'd had to stop and talk to him and would be later than the other cops on their way up. But not too fast. They couldn't let it rattle them.

"Don't think he was involved," Jones contributed, a little out of breath as they walked quickly along the uphill slope.

"His reaction seemed pretty genuine. Backed down when he realized there really was something going on. Got scared."

Margie nodded her agreement. His first reaction had been natural, thinking he was being targeted for some reason, that his civil rights were being violated because he was brown-skinned and wearing a hoodie. Not an unusual reaction. Anyone with dark skin was aware of law enforcement's racial biases.

Margie and Jones hurried past beautifully planted gardens filled with colorful lilies and many different flowers Margie couldn't identify by name. On the side of the hill was a round garden planted with white and red flowers forming a Canada flag. It was probably a nice, peaceful place early in the morning before the crowds with children showed up or drones were flown toward the airport. She looked out at the horizon, but couldn't see the airport from there. It was close, but not that close.

"Just over there," Jones said, pointing in a slightly different direction, understanding what Margie was looking for. "If they hadn't shut down the air traffic, you would see commercial flights taking off and flying over the park every few minutes. Really close. You aren't allowed to fly anything here. Not even a kite or helium balloon."

"Why would anyone fly a drone from here to the airport? What is the point? Are they trying to make a threat? To see how close they can get before they are noticed? Is it just some kids pulling a prank or something serious?"

"I don't know." Jones pressed her lips together in a thin line and shook her head. "Probably just a prank. People do stupid things and then can't understand why everyone gets upset."

Margie chuckled. "That's true," she admitted. She'd seen plenty of it in her time both as a patrol officer and as a detective. People did incredibly stupid and dangerous things for no reason at all. One impulsive move could result in all kinds of trouble.

They got to a flatter area and tried to catch their breaths. There were a couple of park benches beside the trail. Margie frowned at them.

"What?" Jones asked, following her eyes. "That guy?" She indicated, with a slight nod, the man sitting on one of the benches.

"No, it's just…" Margie's brows knit as she looked at the benches, "Why are the benches on the outside of the park, looking down at a feeder road rather than toward the green space and gardens? Who wants to look at the backs of warehouses and semis driving down a dusty road?"

Jones laughed. "I don't know. Doesn't make much sense. But ask him!" They moved toward the man to advise him that he needed to move along.

"Excuse me, sir," Margie called out. "You need to head back to the parking lot. The park is being closed due to a public safety issue."

There was no movement or response from the man facing away from them, apparently entranced with the warehouse traffic.

"Sir!" Margie stepped closer. The man had obviously not heard her at all, not cocking his head or turning to hear her more clearly. He was probably either hard of hearing or wearing earbuds. She stepped around the bench so that he would see that she was trying to talk to him. "Sir, I said—"

She cut herself off and stared.

CHAPTER FOUR

"What is it?" Jones asked, reading trouble in Margie's face.

"We've got another problem," Margie said, waiting for Jones to come around the bench and see for herself.

It was the classic dramatic moment of a cop TV show. The police coming up on a sitting man to find that he was not staring out at the traffic, or sleeping, or rocking out to some tunes on his earbuds. Instead, his eyes were dull, his shirt red with blood, and his skin already gray.

Jones looked at him and echoed Margie's sentiment. She pulled out her cell phone and tapped the screen, putting it on speaker for the call.

"Find something?" MacDonald demanded, his voice sharp. "Where are you?"

"We are at a park bench on the west path," Jones announced, "looking down at... I think it's Westwinds Drive. We have a dead body."

There was silence from MacDonald. Whatever choice words he had, he kept in his head, demonstrating great restraint in front of his team.

"What's the situation?" MacDonald questioned after a long pause. "Do we have an active shooter? Is he the drone pilot? Just what little nest of rattlesnakes have we disturbed here?"

"Hard to tell, sir," Jones said, studying the man on the bench. "He looks… like a businessman. Maybe a salesperson or technician. Neat, collared shirt, khakis. Late twenties to early thirties, white."

"Can't tell whether it is a gunshot wound or a knife," Margie contributed. "We haven't touched anything, and his jacket is covering the wound. But there's a good amount of blood. There's no controller here, so I wouldn't peg him as the drone pilot. I could be wrong, but I would guess no."

"The two of you hold the scene," MacDonald instructed. "We will finish reconnoitering and come to your location with tape and whatever else is needed. I'll put a call out for the medical examiner's office now, but I don't know who else we will need. Have you seen any sign of the pilot or launch zone?"

Margie did a slow 360-degree turn, looking for any trampled or worn ground, but she didn't see any indication that anyone other than the victim had been there. Except, of course, for the fact that he didn't appear to have killed himself.

"I don't see anything," she offered. "You?"

Jones shook her head. "Me neither. But if it was just a little drone, like we used at Edworthy Park, then you don't need anything special to launch it. No launchpad or runway. They just go straight up like a helicopter, and they wouldn't be heavy enough to leave any trace on the ground."

"That's true," Margie agreed. "Have we heard anything else about the size or shape of the drone at the airport? What kind of space they would have needed to launch it?"

"I've seen some blurred pictures, but nothing very good

yet," MacDonald said. "Let's say… between the size of a Bankers Box and a large dog kennel. With a carbon fiber body, probably between twenty-five to fifty pounds. Depending on whether there was any kind of payload."

Margie shook her head. "It could have taken off from anywhere in the park. I don't think it would show any trace in the grass, and if it did, it could take off from one of the gravel or paved pathways without leaving a mark. Something that small and light…"

"It would have to use a drone launchpad or a level concrete path." Margie recognized Siever's voice over the phone. "It has to take off on a level surface, and you want a pad to prevent any gravel or other debris from being kicked up by the rotors. But the pad folds down to… about a foot square. Easy to carry in and out of the park. The drone itself would be more cumbersome and obvious."

"Anywhere the grass has been flattened by a pad?" MacDonald asked, though his tone suggested that he expected the answer to be no. Margie had already said there was no obvious trampling of the grass.

Margie looked around again, but couldn't see any regular shapes that had been pressed down into the grass. She assumed a launchpad would be either a circle or a square.

"No, I don't see anything like that. Maybe you'll be able to see something from the top of the hill."

"We're already there, and I don't see anything like that." MacDonald didn't sound too happy about it. Margie didn't imagine he was pleased about dragging his team all the way over there to look for bent grass or other signs of the drone, launchpad, or pilot, only to find nothing.

"Well… there's no guarantee that this homicide is connected with the drone launch, but I would say there is a pretty good chance," Margie pointed out. "The odds of two unusual crimes happening at the same park simultaneously and being unrelated to each other seem pretty low. They must be related, somehow."

"That's true," MacDonald agreed. "So maybe we don't have the pilot or any direct evidence of the launch, but we have something. Maybe that will get us closer to the identity of the pilot or the motive for the drone being flown to the airport."

"That's right," Margie agreed. "And it is obviously something that the pilot feels strongly about. So the motive shouldn't be too hard to figure out."

"You two stay put," MacDonald instructed them. "We'll get to you as soon as we can. Maybe something else will come up in the meantime. A witness, missing person report, update from the airport. There are a lot of moving parts right now. Sorry you get the 'exciting' part."

"Uh, yeah, thanks," Jones said dryly. "Someone owes me coffee now. Everybody else gets a treasure hunt, and we get to babysit the dead guy."

"Owes *us* coffee," Margie corrected.

"You'll get it," MacDonald promised. "Eventually."

He terminated the call. Jones slid the phone back away. She put her hands in her pockets and sighed, looking around.

CHAPTER FIVE

*I*t was some time before the rest of the team finished their "treasure hunt," coming up dry for any evidence that the drone had launched from the park.

MacDonald walked over to the two detectives at the bench with the corpse, mincing and putting his feet down carefully one at a time, always looking before setting it down to make sure that he wasn't stepping on any evidence. No wrappers, cigarettes, bent blades of grass, or anything else that might tell part of the story of what had happened to their victim. He gazed at the dead man without touching him, just as Margie and Jones had done. He shook his head.

"He knew something," he concluded. "This man knew something about what went down here today. Did he sit down here to watch the drone launch? To talk to someone about it? Did he launch it, and then someone else took all of the evidence away? Why did they do it?" He stared off toward the airport, then down at the street below them, with constant traffic from cars and semis. "Who set these benches facing this direction, anyway? Shouldn't they be facing in to the park?"

"Don't know," Margie admitted. "My guess is that whoever installed the anchors put them in backward. I can't imagine anyone actually thought someone would sit here watching the traffic."

"It might have been installed for plane spotters," MacDonald suggested.

"Plane spotters?"

"You've never heard the term before? People who like to watch planes take off and land."

"Well… I can see how some people would enjoy it, but…?"

MacDonald smiled slightly. "But who would like to do it that much? You could say the same about people who collect stamps or coins. Or who cheer for a particular football team. Everyone has their own interests and hobbies, and some people like planes."

"And they would just sit here…" Margie stood in front of the bench, facing the airport, "and watch airplanes take off all day?"

"Maybe not all day. Maybe just for a few hours."

"Huh."

Margie had seen plenty of planes take off and land when she lived in Winnipeg. It hadn't been that enthralling. She'd been excited when, as a kid, she had seen the Canadian Forces Snowbirds, well-known for their formation flying and aerobatic displays. They were sometimes booked for events like football openers, and everyone cheered them on when they came. And Margie had been dragged to the Royal Aviation Museum as part of a school field trip, which had been interesting for about five minutes, and thereafter, mind-numbingly boring.

Margie guessed she just wasn't an airplane person.

The other detectives strung up the yellow perimeter tape to prevent anyone from contaminating the scene, but the park had already been evacuated, so there probably wasn't any real need for it. There were way too many detectives for one homicide scene, so after making sure Margie and Jones didn't need anything else, MacDonald dismissed the rest of the unit. The patrol officers would keep the parking lot closed and prevent anyone from entering the park. Margie anticipated other inspectors from the airport or NAV CANADA might want to look around the park for any evidence they might have missed.

MacDonald headed back to the office, leaving Margie and Jones to wait for a representative from the Office of the Chief Medical Examiner's office to show up to examine the body in situ before taking it back to the morgue for a post-mortem. The sun was getting lower in the western sky when the van from OCME finally showed up. The van drove most of the way up the pathway they had walked in on before pulling to a stop. The medical examiner and an assistant disembarked and walked carefully over to the bench.

Margie nodded at Dr. Galt, who she knew from several other homicide cases. His white goatee was neatly trimmed. He gave her a cheerful smile.

"Ah, Detective Parks Pat," he greeted her. "Back in your element, I see."

Margie shook her head. "Apparently so. At least this time, I was the first one on the scene and didn't have to make everyone wait." She glanced at Jones. "Except for Detective Jones, of course."

"Well, that was very kind of you. And how are you, Detective Jones?"

Jones shifted her feet. There was no hiding that she was exhausted, having spent too long on her feet without having the opportunity to sit down anywhere. There was a bench right in front of them, but she couldn't use it. MacDonald had left them with a couple of bottles of water so they wouldn't get too dehydrated while waiting, but that just meant needing to trade off while one ran to the washroom and the other kept the scene secure.

"I'm ready to go home," Jones confessed. "As soon as you and the evidence techs finish the scene…"

"Well, it shouldn't be too long now," he assured her. "The techs are already in the parking lot. So once I have a chance to look over the scene…" He looked down at the man on the bench. "Seems pretty straightforward. Anyone touched him?"

Margie and Jones shook their heads. "No."

"Didn't take his pulse?"

Margie shrugged. "Looked like he'd been dead for a while. I didn't feel the need to touch him."

"What time did you get here?"

Margie looked at the time on her phone. "Three o'clock, maybe."

"And you think he had already been dead for a few hours at that point?"

"His skin had lost its color. Eyes were cloudy."

Galt nodded. He worked with the body, moving it around, checking for rigor mortis, temperature, and the origin of all of the blood.

"Shot or stabbed?" Jones inquired.

"Stabbed." Galt considered, looking around. "Much quieter. I imagine there were probably a number of people in the park at midday."

"There were quite a few here when we arrived," Margie agreed. "And no one even noticed."

"From the pathway, you can't tell anything is wrong," Galt pointed out. "It isn't until you get around in front of him, and it would be pretty intrusive just to come and stand in front of him, especially if it is someone you don't know. Very rude."

Even Margie and Jones had not done that, calling out to

him and trying to warn him of their presence before talking to him, trying to get his attention before going around the bench to talk to him.

"You're probably right. And there isn't exactly anyone playing Frisbee over here," Jones acknowledged. There wasn't really anything to do by the bench. Only to sit down and look out at the traffic or toward the airport. Maybe guiding a drone.

"Do you think anyone would notice if a drone took off from here?" Margie asked Dr. Galt.

"With my great knowledge of drones?" he asked dryly. He looked around. "I have no idea. How big?"

Margie made an approximation with her hands. Holding them a meter and a half apart. Galt looked around.

"I don't imagine they can take off from the side of the hill. Maybe down there, behind the washrooms," he pointed to the flat area on the other side of the hill, the back side of the park. "If no one was playing on the fields or doing any landscaping work, there probably wouldn't be anyone nearby. You could sit up here and control it, fly it over the low buildings there and over the major roadways. At that point, people will see it, but if they don't see where it took off from, they won't know where the pilot is…"

Margie studied the angles and nodded, thinking that it was possible. "Are there any other entrances? Other than the main parking lot?"

"There usually are. Maintenance entrances, if nothing else. And there isn't usually much security, even if there is a gate. Maybe a chain and a padlock; most of the time, the padlock isn't even closed; it's just for show. You should be able to get a map of the park that shows all entrances. There's no guarantee that the pilot came in by the main entrance. If there is one down there… he might have been able to avoid detection while he set the drone up."

It took some skill to walk or drive into a park full of people with a drone and not even be spotted.

"There might still be security cameras," Jones said. "We'll have to get all of the footage we can from the entrances, any nearby traffic cams, and store security video."

CHAPTER SIX

a roaring noise filled Margie's ears, and she and the others looked up at the sky to see a jet plane taking off. It was low in the sky and had obviously just left the airport. Despite what the others had already said about it being a good place for plane spotting and a protected airspace, Margie was still surprised at how close it was.

"I guess that means they have resolved the drone issue," Jones observed. "They've started allowing flights out."

"I guess so!" Margie agreed. She just stood there tracking it over their heads for a minute. "I can see why people come here to watch the planes."

Jones grinned. "Right?"

Galt finished his preliminary examination of the body and pulled a wallet out of the man's jacket pocket with gloved hands. He flipped it open. Margie got closer to look at the man's operator's license. The face on the plastic card, serious, glasses, clean-shaven, with neat brown hair, was a match to the man who sat before them on the bench.

"Xander Cartier," Galt announced.

"That's quite the name," Jones chuckled. "Who names their kid Xander?"

"Mr. and Mrs. Cartier, apparently," Margie offered. "Any idea who he is or what he does?" she asked Dr. Galt.

He flipped over the section of the wallet containing the identity card to look behind it, and shook his head. "We will remove and itemize each of his cards at the office. Photos will be uploaded to the shared workspace so you can look at them and do your background checks."

Looking at the top slice of each card that was visible, Margie didn't see anything unusual. Mostly bank or credit cards. There would be enough information in the wallet to be get a search warrant for his house, run a criminal background search, a credit check, to find the license plate and description of his current vehicle—which might still be parked in a nearby street or parking lot—and hopefully, to track down his family to inform them of his passing.

Would any of this information shed light on why Xander had been on that bench—or why he'd met his end there? That remained to be seen.

"Anything else in his pockets?" Jones asked.

Galt patted them and shook his head. "We will itemize everything, but there doesn't appear to be anything else significant."

"No phone?" Margie asked.

Galt shook his head slowly. "Notably absent."

Another plane roared overhead. The first had barely passed over the park. Margie supposed they would be sending them out as quickly as possible, trying to catch up after keeping the flights delayed for several hours. She felt bad for the people who had been sitting on the runway the whole time. At least the people who hadn't boarded yet had access to a food court and washrooms and could get up and move around. She didn't imagine waiting in the aircraft on the runway had been very comfortable.

"Is there anything else we need to do here?"

"We'll get the crime scene techs over to take some pictures before and after removing the body," Galt said, "And then we will release the scene to you. It doesn't look like there will be much evidence to recover other than the body. One of you might want to check outside the perimeter to see if the phone was thrown down the hill or into a garbage can."

Margie was eager to move around, and Jones looked dead on her feet. "I'll take a look around," she volunteered. "You can stay here while the crime scene techs do their thing."

CHAPTER SEVEN

*I*t was another hour before everybody agreed that they had done all they could with what was at the scene. Dr. Galt and his assistant bagged and removed Mr. Cartier's body. Other than wiping down the bench so the next visitor didn't end up sitting in a smear of dried, powdered blood, there wasn't anything else to do. Plane after plane streaked across the sky. Margie knew that YYC was one of the busiest airports in Canada, but she had never stopped to consider just how many flights went in and out every day.

She and Jones walked back to their cars.

"Do you want me to lead you home?" Jones offered, sweeping a couple of curls of blond hair away from her face and trying ineffectually to tuck them back into a bobby pin.

"No, no," Margie protested. Her house was in a completely different part of the city from Jones's, who lived in Sunnyside. "It's way out of your way. I'm usually pretty good at getting home using GPS. I'll be fine once I get to a street I recognize."

"The best way from here is probably Barlow Trail or Fifty-Second Street."

Margie would have to take her word for it. She didn't want to try to take directions from Jones, which might conflict with what the GPS said and confuse her. "I'll be fine. Thanks."

They said goodbye and got into their respective vehicles. Margie mounted her phone and told the maps app to take her home, and managed to get home without any difficulty. The sun was getting close to the horizon, spreading golden streaks across the sky, and she knew that she was late for her movie marathon with Christina. They might only be able to get one movie or a couple of TV shows now. After figuring out what to do for supper.

She had given Christina a heads-up while waiting for Dr. Galt, so it wouldn't be a surprise that Margie was so late getting home. Christina grudgingly accepted that she wasn't always in charge of her own schedule and couldn't control when people got murdered or launched drones at the airport.

Margie pulled to the curb in front of the house. When she got to the door, she heard Stella's collar jangling, and by the time she got the door open, Stella was racing toward her, barking a happy greeting. Margie bent over to greet her and to scratch the delighted dog's brown ears and chin, talking doggie talk to her.

"Who's a good girl? Yes, yes, I love you too. Who's my good girl, Stella?"

After giving her eager dog enough love to settle her down, Margie looked at Christina, who stood watching her, arms folded across her chest, waiting for her turn.

"And who's my other good girl?" Margie asked with a laugh.

"Hi. I wasn't expecting you to be so late." Christina gathered her long black hair and pulled it back so it all fell behind her shoulders.

"Yes. I'm sorry about that. It took the ME longer than I

expected to get there. Unfortunately, I can't rush these things. Just have to wait for everyone to finish their parts of the investigation at their own speed."

"I know," Christina sighed. "Heard it all before."

"I'm sorry, honey. I was looking forward to coming home and spending time with you watching the movies." Margie looked at her watch. "We can still—"

"It's not a movie marathon if you only watch one movie," Christina dismissed. "You can put on whatever you want, and we'll try to do the Batman marathon another day. Maybe you can fit it in on Saturday or Sunday. If nobody gets murdered."

"Yes… I hope so. Do you have any plans for the weekend that I need to work around?"

"Tracy and I need to study for a social studies test. It will depend on when he is free. He has to work for his parents sometimes."

"Okay. We'll work around whatever time he has so you guys still have time to study." Margie sniffed the air. "Something smells good! What did you make?"

Christina rolled her eyes. "Bannock. It was fresh about three hours ago. Like I said, I didn't think you would take so long. The stuff about the drone at the airport ended ages ago. Everything is 'back to normal operations' again."

"We saw a lot of airplanes flying out of there. The park is right under their flight path. Or at least under today's weather conditions. I guess if the wind is blowing a different direction, they probably take a different path. I'm sorry I wasn't here when it was hot off the grill. But can I still have some?" Margie put a little pleading in her voice. "You know how much I love your bannock."

Christina allowed a little smile at that. "Of course. I don't expect you to starve. I left you some."

"Awesome." Margie removed her shoes and left them on

the mat beside the door. She wiggled her toes, glad to finally have them free of the constricting shoes. She wore comfortable shoes but had been standing and walking around the park for a long time. Stella came over to shove her nose into each shoe and get more loves from Margie, then escorted her into the kitchen and sat woefully beside her bowl of kibble as if it were empty.

"Oh, I don't think you're starving," Margie told her. "You've got plenty of food there if you were really hungry."

"She had her canned food already," Christina agreed. "Don't let her snow you."

Margie washed up at the kitchen sink and started pulling leftovers and condiments from the fridge to accompany her bannock. She fed Stella a little piece of buttered bannock when she didn't think Christina was watching, but Christina caught her.

"Don't give the dog people food," she reprimanded, echoing what Margie had been telling Christina since she was a toddler.

Margie chuckled. "You weren't supposed to see that."

Christina sat down at the table, her body relaxing and her mood starting to soften.

"I guess it ended up being a pretty busy day," she observed.

"Yes, a lot longer than I had expected. People should check with me before they go getting murdered."

"That would be the polite thing to do," Christina agreed. She reached over to the counter to grab a piece of bannock for herself.

Margie took a bite and savored the sweet, buttery flavor.

"And how was school?" Margie asked.

"Oh… you know. Just trying to get along… figure out how people will get their diplomas after a year of COVID, that kind of thing. It's all kind of crazy. The teachers don't really know. Some of them say it will all work out, that the administration will be fair about the number of credits required and about grades dropping during the lockdown and all of that. Others say we have to get our butts in gear and catch up and ace the finals and take summer school to bump up our credits." She rolled her eyes and sighed. "The whole world has gone crazy."

"I know," Margie agreed. "It's been pretty crazy for everyone. But I feel especially bad for high school students. There was enough pressure when I was in school. Adding all of the fear, social distancing, distance learning, and everything else has made it much more difficult."

"How *did* you graduate from high school?" Christina asked.

Margie shifted uncomfortably. This wasn't something that she had discussed with Christina before, even though the opportunity had presented itself more than once. Margie always focused on Christina and her circumstances, rather than referring to what had happened to her and how she had or hadn't succeeded in handling it. But she supposed that sooner or later, they were bound to have an open and frank discussion about it.

"Well, I got pregnant with you while I was still in high school. There were some community programs for pregnant teens, but I wasn't very… together at that point. I was mad at my mom and didn't want to listen to anything she said or do anything she thought I should do."

"Why?"

"Things weren't great at home. I didn't always have all of the things that you do. And in Manitoba, the area I was in… there was a lot of really nasty prejudice against Indians. Even though we were such a high percentage of the population, we were second-class citizens. At least in the places I lived. So there were things inside and outside the home that made me really angry."

"Did your mom abuse you?"

Margie swallowed. She arranged the food on her plate with great precision, staying focused on that rather than looking at Christina.

"Parenting was different then from what it is now. Good parents smacked their kids. It wasn't looked down on like it is now. It is hard to find a defined edge between appropriate corporal punishment and abuse."

"So you were smacked," Christina said flatly.

"Yes. Sometimes. No more than any of my friends. At least, I don't think so. It isn't like we talked to each other and compared notes. But you did know the kids who really got whipped or were afraid of their parents. Anyway... when I got pregnant, I didn't want to stay home, and I didn't want to stay in a group home or foster family. I wanted to be a grown-up, but I wasn't ready to be one. I went through a difficult time."

"And then you had me," Christina said, giving Margie the grace to gloss over those wretched months and move on in her story.

"And then I had you," Margie agreed. She smiled at Christina. "What a shriveled-up little purple prune you were."

They both laughed. Margie had mentioned Christina's newborn appearance to her before.

"And I fell in love," Margie said simply. "You were the most perfect, most innocent creature on earth, and you were mine. So I cleaned up my act. I stopped fighting against the case workers and everyone else who had been trying to get me into a stable situation and to apply for the benefits I would need to grow up and take care of myself and you. I got into a shelter for girls like me, which had a daycare program, while I went to adult education programs to get me ready to take the GED. And I got it the first time I tried. That was... a really challenging way to go about getting my diploma." She raised her brows at Christina. "I wouldn't recommend it."

"I'm not going to get pregnant," Christina declared. "I wouldn't do that. I know what you did must have been really hard. It made you tough, so you could go to school to become a cop."

"Yes," Margie agreed. "And trust me, there are not a lot of Indigenous single moms lining up to go through the police academy. Not a lot of brown or black people apply to be cops in Winnipeg. Even fewer of them make it through. And even once you have graduated and are part of the rank and file, there are still a lot of people trying to get you to quit. People inside the force and out. Lots of pressure to give up and get out."

"Why don't people want us to be cops? If so many people who get in trouble with the law are Native, then why don't they want us to help with the policing?"

"They figure we should only be First Nations police. White people don't like to be policed by brown people. But for the bands with their own police... that's really hard too. Not hard to get into, but hard to get any respect from their own people or the white law enforcement. And Métis don't have their own separate police force, even if that was what I'd wanted to do."

Margie picked up a piece of bannock and nibbled it. She had managed to stick with it in the Winnipeg Police Department, despite the people who had wanted to push her out. And she had managed to get a position in Calgary without relying on the "diversity card." She was definitely more accepted in Calgary than she had ever been in Manitoba.

"Will you be able to advance in Calgary?" Christina asked. "Or is detective as far as you can go?"

"I don't know," Margie admitted. "I don't see Indigenous people in any positions of authority. But that doesn't mean there won't ever be. I'm going to try. I'm going to apply for positions just like any white man in the ranks. And a few more years down the line… who knows?"

Christina nodded. She called Stella to her and scratched her ears and head.

"What do *you* want to do?" Margie asked. "Do you have any idea? It's okay if you don't. A lot of kids go to a couple of years of university before they decide what they want to be."

"Maybe science," Christina said, not looking at her. "I don't know yet. I like that stuff, but I know it's really hard for girls—for women—in university and the workforce. And Indigenous women…" She shrugged dramatically. "I'm just not sure. And my math and science marks aren't the best, especially with the move and COVID."

"It's okay not to be sure. It's a tough world out there. Just take one step at a time. Try to work with the system to get your diploma. Even if it takes a year longer because of COVID."

CHAPTER EIGHT

*M*argie was exhausted, but even after eating dinner and watching a couple of shows with Christina before bed, she found it hard to settle. Her mind whirled as she thought about Christina and the challenges she faced as a woman, an Indigenous person, and a COVID-era student. Not to mention being transplanted to Calgary during her teen years, which she had not been happy about. Her friendship with Tracy made it easier to get her to go to school and to accept that her life was now in Calgary, at least until she graduated and decided where she wanted to go next in life.

Thank goodness for a steady, mature, academic friend like Tracy. Margie had not been happy with the crowd Christina had been running with in "the Peg." When they had moved to Calgary, Margie had been worried that Christina might even run away and return to Manitoba on her own, choosing to live with a friend or in a shelter rather than being forced to live in Calgary.

When Margie wasn't worrying about Christina and the

challenges and life choices she was going to face in the next couple of years, her mind returned to the drone and the investigation into Xander Cartier's murder.

They had to be related. Margie was sure of that. But how? She would need to know a lot more about Cartier before speculating about that. All she knew now was that he was a young, clean-cut man who didn't look like he had ever committed a crime in his life. Maybe he had shoplifted a chocolate bar when he was five, and the guilt of that had placed him on the right side of the law from then on.

Why had the drone been flown into the YYC airspace? It didn't make any sense. Whoever had done it had known that it would be seen and that YYC security, the police, the RCMP, and NAV CANADA would take measures to make sure it was taken down and could not do any harm while it was in the restricted flight zone. If it had been carrying any ordnance, she would have heard about it by now. On the news, if not through official channels. If it had just been a mischievous prank, Xander Cartier would not be dead. Silly teenagers who decided on a whim they could get away with aiming a drone toward the airport would be sitting in jail by now, waiting for their parents to pick them up.

Then why fly a drone into the restricted airspace?

Margie tossed and turned, trying to make sense of it all, and then pushed it out of her mind and resumed worrying about Christina.

By morning, Margie didn't feel like she'd slept more than a couple of hours. But that was what coffee was for. She made herself a big travel mug as soon as she got up, and she would have more when she hit the office, if she needed it. It might result in an emotional dip in the afternoon, but hopefully, by then, they would know something about what had happened to Xander and who was involved in the drone launch, and they would be conducting interviews or knocking on doors. Something active that would keep her body and mind occupied instead of falling asleep over her keyboard.

Christina was not up yet, so Margie let Stella out for a quick run in the yard and stood on the back steps sipping her coffee. But Christina was at that point in her life when sleeping late was more important than getting up to say goodbye to her mother or having a long shower before school. Hair and makeup could be done on the bus on the way to school and breakfast would probably be an oily muffin from the cafeteria. Christina could be out of bed and ready for the bus in ten minutes, and her series of wake-up alarms was precisely timed.

Margie was not the first one into the office, but she wasn't the last. Most of the team looked just as puffy eyed as Margie did, a testament to the fact that they had also been tossing and turning trying to figure out the puzzling new cases on the board.

MacDonald had texted a notice to the team that he expected them to be there and ready for a stand-up meeting at eight o'clock. Earlier than usual. The techs had probably been up all night processing evidence, and there would be a briefing from the airport as to what they had found out about the drone and its origin. Dr. Galt probably would not have done the postmortem yet, but would be conducting it this morning.

Margie was assembled with everyone else by eight o'clock, coffee mugs in nearly every person's grip, when MacDonald walked into the room to begin the meeting.

He looked around the room to ensure everyone was there, nodded, and began.

"I'm sure you have all been watching the news coverage

of the drone incident yesterday and trying to figure out how much of the reporting is true and what is speculation. So here's the word. All the investigating agencies agree the drone was launched from Prairie Winds Park. Detectives Jones and Patenaude have some ideas of where the drone might have been brought in and launched from. We have feet on the ground following up on those details, canvassing for any surveillance video confirming or refuting their theory."

He nodded in Margie's direction to acknowledge their contribution.

"The drone was brought down on one of the runways by the Airport RCMP Detachment, using wireless technology."

"They spoofed it?" Siever inquired. "Took over the controls from the pilot?"

MacDonald looked at him and shrugged. "I'm sure you can find the details in the joint briefing document issued by the RCMP and NAV CANADA. The technology is beyond me. I still rely on my kid to program my PVR when he is home for the holidays."

There was a rumble of laughter from the rest of the detectives. Siever's cheeks turned pink and he looked down at his papers, nodding.

"What do we know about the drone? Aside from the technical stuff?" Cruz asked. Siever looked toward him and nodded, indicating his interest in this question as well.

"You can find the make and model in the documents. There was no payload—no explosives, weaponry, or delivery device. Out of the box, this model is outfitted for filming. Used by the motion picture industry, mapping, and hobbyists for various applications."

"Out of the box?" Cruz repeated. "Can we assume that it was modified, then? Did it have a camera when it flew into YYC?"

"If it did, it could be advance surveillance for some other operation," Jones suggested. "A heist or terrorist threat."

"We can't rule it out. It did have a camera, which, from what I understand, did not have long-range broadcasting capability. If it was broadcasting to someone, they had to be close by. NAV is trying to replicate the drone's flight path during the entire time it was active yesterday, so they have a picture of exactly what it could have filmed. So far, they don't believe that it acquired any sensitive information. But there are concerns about what had been planned for the return trip."

The room was silent enough to hear a pin drop. Nobody said, "Return trip?" but of course, it was what everybody was thinking. MacDonald looked around at everyone's faces, but still, no one spoke. He looked back down at the papers on the table before him.

"The most concerning thing at the moment is the ballast the drone was carrying. As well as the standard video equipment this drone is built for, it had been modified to carry another one hundred pounds of ballast. It would appear that this was an initial test to see if that much weight could be carried from Prairie Winds Park into the airport."

They all looked at each other, considering the possibilities.

"So what weighs one hundred pounds?" Jones mused.

"Enough Semtex to blow up an entire city block," Gagnon suggested.

They all looked at him, but nobody challenged the suggestion.

"An automatic weapon with armor-piercing bullets," Cruz contributed.

"It isn't necessarily a weapon," Margie pointed out. "It could be more movie equipment. With a longer transmission range, higher quality, or some other specification for which they need more weight."

"One hundred and fifty pounds," Siever argued.

Everyone looked at him questioningly.

"It was only one hundred pounds of ballast," MacDonald said sternly. "Unless you have updated information that I haven't seen yet."

"It had a hundred pounds of ballast and fifty pounds of camera equipment. If it didn't need a camera for the return trip, it could be a payload of one hundred fifty pounds."

They all looked at each other, nodding. Of course Siever was correct. They didn't know if whatever the pilot had planned would require a camera or not. The modified drone had the ability to carry one hundred and fifty pounds.

"It could be a person," Margie said. "They could be trying to get a person over the fence at the airport."

"What for?" MacDonald asked.

"I don't know," she admitted. "It would get a person past the airport's security measures. There have been a number of heists that have been committed at airports just by driving a van through a security fence and grabbing what they want as it is being loaded or unloaded. You could do the same by dropping someone over the fence. They could run in and grab… whatever."

"And how would they get out?" Gagnon demanded. "Then the drone needs to be able to lift one hundred and fifty pounds plus whatever they are stealing."

"Diamonds don't weigh much. We might not get a lot of diamonds through YYC, but the diamond mining operations in the Northwest Territories ship a lot of product out through Yellowknife. Just because they tested the drone here, that doesn't mean they will use it here. They could use it in another airport under similar conditions. This could be a test run *and* misdirection. They might have been planning to hit another airport while we were still chasing our tails here."

She looked around at the other detectives, who were thinking about it but didn't come up with any questions or arguments against it.

"Some of the most successful airport heists in Canada have been gold. But gold *is* heavy. You could have a light thief and fifty pounds of gold, which is not a bad haul, but not much more than that."

"How far could it go with that kind of payload?" Cruz asked, raising his hand slightly before voicing the question, like a kid in school. "They tested to make sure it could go from Prairie Winds Park to the airport, but say it goes over the fence, the thief grabs whatever it is, and then... how much battery or fuel does it have left? How far can it go to get safely away? And how does it get away without being tracked?"

They considered these questions. Margie still thought that a heist was a possibility. As long as the airport didn't have a drone on standby to chase after it, they would be relying on the control tower's radar limitations and human sightings. Airport radar couldn't track a drone if it were close to the ground, could it? The thieves would only need to have a vehicle waiting on the other side of the fence or within a kilometer or so of the airport. If the pilot were operating the drone without any video capabilities, then he needed to keep it in sight. He needed to be close by, and then could grab the payload and run.

"A lot of things to consider," MacDonald said finally. "We will need to do a lot more investigating to figure out what they were planning if we want to be able to foil a real attack. There will be equipment to be traced, as well as a deep dive into Xander Cartier and how he might be connected to the operation. Was he just an innocent bystander who saw more than he should have? Was he part of the crew that planned this incursion? Or was he fighting against it?"

"We must know who his family or friends are by this point," Margie said. "Dr. Galt had his name and address yesterday. He should have some suggestions on how to reach the next of kin by now."

"Maybe. If not, I'm sure we can track them down pretty quickly ourselves. Are you volunteering to do the death notification, Detective Pat?"

"Sure. I can give the death notification, have a look around, ask whether we can see his room or residence, if they know of anyone else who should be informed, his employer, whatever else we can get out of them."

MacDonald nodded. "Good. You're always good at that sort of contact. Who do you want to take with you?"

Margie glanced over their faces. Jones or Cruz were the best options. Both were good with people and would be sympathetic. Some of the other team members would not make the same favorable impression.

"Can I wait until we have some sense of who the next of kin is before I pick someone?" she asked. Cruz would be the best in some situations, and Jones in others. Age, race, and gender were all factors to be considered.

"That's fine. Just grab someone when you are ready. Everybody should be here unless they are actively tracking down a lead in one of these two cases. Understood?" He looked around the room.

Everyone nodded. No one would be working on cold cases or less important jobs today. They would run down every lead they could for a few days, and not back off until the leads on the drone and Cartier cases started to run dry.

MacDonald nodded. His tight "wrapping it up" nod. "Detective Pat is in charge of the death notification and any information that flows into or out of it. And Detective Siever, you are taking point on the drone?"

Siever nodded eagerly. "Yes, sir. Happy to."

"Everyone else, we are looking for video footage, social media posts, and any chatter about what happened at the park and the airport. Check in with informants. We need to dig down and find out what is going on here. That's it. Dismissed."

CHAPTER NINE

*X*ander Cartier.

Who was Xander Cartier?

A quick search of the system told Margie that he didn't have a criminal record. At least not under that name. OCME would put his fingerprints and any other identifying details into the system in case he had an alias. She would search for a legal name change. She assumed that his license had been legitimate. It had looked good at first glance, none of the red flags Margie had been trained to look for.

She ran through the various other systems she could search, coming across his name with vital statistics, a motor vehicles search, and land titles office. He was young, but apparently well enough off to buy a house of his own. These days, that was something many twenty-somethings could not afford. Or even thirty-somethings. Margie had worked hard to be able to buy her first house in Manitoba, and it was sad to think that Christina might not be able to do the same thing until she was much older. Especially in a major center like Calgary. Young people with families often had to buy or build outside the city.

She searched for Xander's parents' names, pulled from his birth certificate, and found they were still living and listed at the same address.

Cartier was a rich-sounding name, but Margie hadn't been sure what to expect when she jumped into the background search. A look at Xander's parents' address and the profile that showed up when she did an internet search for his father's business showed that her first impression had been correct. The Cartiers were as well-monied as their name suggested. His father was the in-house lawyer for one of the big oil firms. But Xander had not followed in his footsteps. There was no LLB or other legal degree after his name, nor did he work for the same company.

Internet searches for Xander Cartier's name only pulled up social media accounts to begin with. His public social media accounts. Margie knew that his generation often had two sets of socials. One for their parents, employers, and other public needs, and other accounts for private use. With luck, she might be able to find a connection between related accounts, but it was tricky.

Diving deeper, Margie gradually turned up other bits of information. Xander seemed to be a programmer or IT support guy. There was not much information about his employer, but he made suggestions on several forums for people with computer issues, sometimes coming up with complex solutions at the end of long "please help me" threads, succeeding where many others had failed.

So Xander was good at what he did. Technologically adept, whether he had university training or experience through other means. A gamer? Hacker? DIY computer builder?

He didn't seem to have an online resume detailing where he worked and his education, which was frustrating.

Eventually, Margie pushed back from her desk. She

looked around the bullpen and caught Cruz's eye as he leaned back, rubbing his eyes. Too much screen time. He would be happy to get away from his desk. He raised his brows at her, and when Margie nodded, he stood up and stretched. Margie got up, and they met by her desk.

"You ready to do the death notification?" Cruz asked.

"Yeah. Father is a bigwig, so I'm thinking we may need someone authoritative to deal with him. He might be unintentionally biased against dealing with a female detective."

"Well, I'd be happy to help out." Cruz glanced around the bullpen at the other men Margie could have picked. But she liked dealing with the friendly Filipino, and he was good with people. She couldn't say the same about everyone else on the team.

Jones gave Margie a look of disappointment as she and Cruz prepared to go, but she didn't voice a protest. They worked a lot of files together, and Jones knew that Margie had to make her decision based on who she thought would get the best results. She lifted her hand in a wave.

"Good luck."

"Thanks."

"You want to visit the father first?" Cruz asked as they climbed into his car. "I gather they will not be in the same place?"

Margie settled comfortably into the passenger seat.

"Yeah. There hasn't been a missing person report filed for him or any inquiries, so I think we can assume they don't know there is anything wrong and are following their usual routines. I'm not sure whether the mother works, but the father definitely does. We'll try his office. If he isn't there, hopefully they can give us his cell number and point us in the right direction. Then he can suggest the best way to approach the mother and break the news to her."

"He'll want to tell her himself, probably."

Margie nodded her agreement. She told him which office tower Mr. Cartier worked at and Cruz didn't need the address or GPS to get him there. He had lived in Calgary for 15 years and knew the city better than a native.

Margie glanced at him as he drove. He was older than she was, a bit of gray salting his black hair. Filipino in origin, he had olive skin, a short, neatly trimmed mustache, and eyes that could be kind or challenging. He was a tough cop, but had the warm heart of a family man, with several children at home.

"You look tired," she observed, noting the puffiness under his eyes that everyone seemed to be sporting today. "You didn't sleep very well last night either?"

He shrugged. "A lot to think about."

Margie nodded. "You think the two cases are related?"

"A drone launch and a murder from the same park at around the same time? Of course they are related."

"That's what I thought too."

"But knowing it and proving it are two different things. We need evidence."

They stopped in front of one of the tall office towers downtown, which actually had a police parking stall out in front. Cruz yelped his siren a few times to get a courier to move out of the space, then pulled in to the curb. The courier looked back and gave him a dirty look, not happy at being kicked out when there were no loading zone spaces free. Cruz didn't even look at him.

They took the elevator up to the company's reception desk and waited for the woman answering and routing phone calls to give them her attention. She had teased blond hair and was probably in her fifties. She looked them over and frowned.

"How can I help you?"

"We need to talk to Mr. Cartier."

"Do you have an appointment?" She looked down at a planner on her desk with tiny lines of cramped writing. "I was not aware he was expecting anyone."

"We don't have an appointment," Margie informed her, stepping closer and lowering her voice to emphasize the gravity of her request. "We are with the Calgary Police and need to speak with him urgently."

"I'm sure whatever it is, it can wait. Mr. Cartier is in a very important meeting."

"There has been a family tragedy. We need to speak to him immediately."

The woman's eyes flickered with interest. She considered this new piece of information. Margie didn't imagine it was a regular occurrence. The receptionist wouldn't have a reference point to determine whether she should interrupt him for this or not.

"I don't know," she waffled. "I'm not supposed to interrupt him. Are you sure this can't wait?"

Margie shook her head. The woman looked at Cruz for his confirmation, and he agreed. "He is going to want to be pulled out for this. I'm sorry to put you in this position, but we really do need to speak to him right now."

The woman eventually nodded. She held up a finger to indicate that they should wait a minute, and punched an extension into her phone. "Sandra, I need you to take a note to Mr. Cartier in the boardroom."

There was an inquiry from the person on the other end, and the receptionist confirmed her request. A young woman walked out to the reception area a minute later. Glasses, hair pulled back away from her face. She looked at the two detectives curiously. The receptionist had written a brief note, and she handed it over to Sandra.

"Take that to Mr. Cartier."

Sandra looked at her one more time for confirmation

that this was really necessary, then nodded and disappeared into the hallway. When she came back a minute later, she was accompanied by the man Margie had seen in photos on the company's website. A heavyset man in an expensive suit. His dark brows were knitted together and he was clearly not happy that his meeting was being interrupted. He didn't take it out on Sandra or the receptionist, though. With his emotions carefully under control, he looked at Margie and Cruz.

"Officers? What is this about?"

"Detectives," Cruz corrected. "We need to talk to you privately."

"I don't understand why I have detectives showing up at my office. If you need to reach out to me, then why not give me a call? What is this about?"

"Can we go to your office or a meeting room?" Cruz insisted.

"Well... fine, yes. I appreciate your discretion." Cartier looked at the receptionist, unsure what directions to give her. He shrugged and turned back away. "I'm sure I won't be long. Maybe take a fresh pot of coffee into the boardroom while they are waiting for me."

She nodded. "Yes, Mr. Cartier."

Cartier flicked a hand at the two detectives to have them follow him. "This way, please."

CHAPTER TEN

*M*argie and Cruz followed him into a small meeting room with a table and four chairs. There was a clean whiteboard on one wall and several upside-down white mugs on a tray waiting to be used. Cartier did not offer them any refreshments. He squeezed into one of the chairs, which was not wide enough to comfortably accommodate his bulk.

"So, what is this about?" he asked.

"You are Xander Cartier's father?" Margie asked.

"Yes." He frowned and shook his head. "Why would you be asking about him? Is he in some kind of trouble?"

"Mr. Cartier, we're here to give you some very bad news. Xander was killed yesterday. He was stabbed by an unknown assailant."

Cartier's jaw dropped open and his face drained of color. He looked around the room, whether for a drink or someone to offer emotional support, Margie didn't know.

"Shot. That doesn't make any sense. He doesn't go to bars or do anything dangerous. Was it an accident? A mugging? Are you sure it was him?"

"We will have his identity verified later. But we have his wallet and driver's license, and his face matches that on the license."

"How is that possible? What happened?" Cartier looked from Margie to Cruz, waiting to be told something that would make sense of the situation.

"We don't have a lot of answers yet, but will tell you what we can," Cruz assured him, and looked over at Margie, directing Cartier's attention back to her. Cartier met Margie's gaze, looking baffled. It hadn't yet hit him that he had really lost his son. The grief wasn't there yet, only shock and confusion. he hadn't expected anything like this.

"Did you hear about the drone that was flown into the YYC airspace yesterday?" she asked.

"Yes. What does that have to do with anything? It didn't seem like anything to be concerned about to me. Just a prank. Some kid pretending he could land a plane at the airport."

"It was more than that, though we don't yet understand what the motive for flying it into the airport was. That drone was launched yesterday from Prairie Winds Park. And that was where I discovered your son's body. There is, so far, nothing to tie him to the drone launch except time and place. We don't know what happened or what he might have witnessed there."

"That's... unfathomable. What was he doing at this park? I don't even know where that is."

"It's not far from the airport. It is in restricted airspace because of the flight path."

"But what was Xander doing there? He should have been at work. He has a job, you know. He isn't some kind of bum or homeless person."

"No. We were not thinking that he was. And it isn't that kind of place. It is a park that is heavily used by families, athletes, and seniors looking for a safe place to walk. It is a popular, clean park, not one that the homeless congregate in. It is also sometimes used by plane spotters, because of the proximity to the airport. There are flights going over there all the time."

"What is all of this about drones and planes? What does that have to do with Xander's death?"

"We don't know. Was he involved in any projects that involved drones? Where did he work?"

"He works for a tech company. I don't know what he does, exactly; it's all a bit beyond me. Way beyond me, if you want the truth. I can do enough to get by on the computer. Send emails, draft and retrieve documents. But I'm not a computer guy. Even phones and tablets… I'm not big on social media. Prefer to find other ways to entertain myself."

Margie suspected that he didn't do much in the way of traditional entertainment. His idea of fun probably involved citing case law or finding a loophole in a contract. She could picture him sitting before his fire during the evening, flipping through a thick stack of paper or opening a five-inch-thick legal tome.

"Do you know the name of his employer?"

"No… my wife would know. She has that information on her phone." He looked suddenly stricken. "My wife. She doesn't know yet?"

"No, sir. We came to you first."

"Good, good." He swallowed hard. "I don't know how I will tell her. She will be devastated. He's our only child." Cartier shook his head in horror. "He *was* our only child. And now he's gone. How could that be? You are sure it is him? It isn't a mistake?"

"We have identified him by his driver's license," Margie reminded him. "We will have official confirmation once we have had a chance to compare fingerprints, dental work, or another biometric."

"Do we need to... go there to identify him?"

"No. You will not need to. Once we are finished, you can have your funeral home pick him up, and you don't have to see him until they have him... prepared. If there were any question of his identity, we would give you a photograph. It would not be like on TV when you have to see him in the morgue, with the sheet pulled back from his face."

Cartier wiped his forehead with the back of his hand. "Dramatic moments," he said, "like the reading of the will. Hollywood stuff."

"Yes, exactly."

"Good. I don't know if we could handle that." He shook his head. "I just can't believe it is true. I can't wrap my head around this. Kids aren't supposed to die before their parents. He didn't do anything dangerous for a living. It isn't like he was in the army. I just... it makes no sense that he is gone."

"We're so sorry, and want you to know that we are putting all of our resources into finding out what happened."

"Thank you. I appreciate that." He rubbed his eyes with his palms. He wasn't crying, but instead looked like he'd had a long night and was trying to wake up. Maybe he was hoping that it was all a nightmare. Margie could only imagine how it must feel to lose his only child, especially when it was so unexpected. She didn't know how she would go on if something happened to Christina.

"Would you like us to drive you home so that you can talk to your wife?" Cruz offered.

"I have my car here. That isn't a problem."

"Do you feel up to driving? You've had a shock, it might not be the best idea," Cruz warned.

"No, no, I'm fine. It hasn't hit yet. I need to get home to my wife. I need to... be with her."

Cruz and Margie nodded.

"Would it be okay if we followed you?" Margie asked. "I know this is not a good time, but if we could get the name of his employer, they should be notified as well. We can take care of that."

"Uh…" he looked at them blankly for a moment, trying to process this. "I suppose. Yes."

"I have your address. Is this correct?" Margie read it to him from her notepad.

"Yes. That's right. Just take… just take Elbow Drive."

Cruz nodded. "I know where it is, sir. Thank you."

"When we get there, do you want us to break the news to your wife while you provide emotional support? Or do you want to do it?" Margie asked.

"I'll tell her," he said immediately. "It should come from me. I appreciate your coming here to tell me in person, but she shouldn't hear it from a stranger. I'll go in first, without you. I'll come to the door and let you in to ask your questions when she is ready."

"Okay. We will wait until you open the door," Margie confirmed. She looked at Cruz. They might be sitting in the car for a while. Mrs. Cartier might not be ready to see them for quite some time. He gave an infinitesimal nod. They could give the Cartiers that time.

"I will walk you out," Mr. Cartier offered. He stood up, pushing himself up out of the constricting chair.

He led the way back to the reception area. He looked at the receptionist and Sandra, both standing by to find out what was going on and when he was going to return to his meeting.

Mr. Cartier touched Sandra's arm, which seemed to surprise her. He spoke to the receptionist, clearly the senior of the two women. "I have to go. Tell the board we will have to reconvene. I don't know when. I've had… a death in the family. I don't know when… I'll be in touch with Linda and give her more details when I have them."

"I'm very sorry, Mr. Cartier," the receptionist's eyes were wide. "You go ahead… and just let us know. I'll inform the others." She looked at her watch. "I'll give you ten minutes to get out of the building first, so no one tries to grab you in the hallway."

He smiled, his lips pale. "That's very considerate. Thank you."

He nodded to Cruz and Margie and retreated to the hallway, going the other way this time. Margie assumed he would need to grab his jacket, briefcase, and any other personal items he would need over the next few days, and to inform Linda, who he assumed was his administrative assistant, why he was leaving.

CHAPTER ELEVEN

"*I*t's not an easy job," Cruz commented when they climbed back into the car.

"No. You see people on the worst days of their lives. Deaths, arrests, medical emergencies… It's no wonder people have negative associations with the police."

"Well, that was handled very professionally. We should be able to get the name of Xander's employer, at least. I doubt the mother will be in a good space to tell us much else."

"Those poor people."

"Don't get too close to it. Maintain a professional distance. You don't need to carry everyone else's trouble around with you. Leave those burdens behind when you go home to Christina."

Margie sighed. She knew he was right. It was difficult. One of the reasons that she was a cop was to help people. "To Protect and to Serve," in the words of the LAPD motto. It was hard not to take other people's grief and pain on herself. But doing so would not help them. They needed her to be under control emotionally to do her best investigative work. And she did need to be able to shut it off at the end of the day.

Most of it, anyway. Cruz showed signs of sleeplessness the night before as he had tried to puzzle out what had happened. He was the more experienced cop, but even he could not shut it *all* off.

Margie pulled out her phone to see if she had received any emails or notices of documents posted to the shared workspace for the drone incident or Cartier files—which so far were being handled as two separate files.

The NAV/RCMP technicians had apparently spent all night disassembling the drone and learning everything they could from the parts that had been modified and the equipment onboard. Margie had assumed that it was a pretty basic piece of machinery. Rotors attached to motors and a battery, and a directional control, with the pilot's remote relaying the flying directions to it wirelessly. She had not considered the possibility of computer chips embedded in it and algorithms making computations and adjustments to deal with the variations in wind speed and direction, motor temperature, and smoothing out the instructions received from the pilot to keep it stable and aloft.

"What are you reading?" Cruz asked.

"Well, they've been taking the drone apart. MacDonald said it had been modified to carry a bigger payload, but that isn't all."

"That was the most obvious thing," Cruz guessed. "Since it was carrying all that extra ballast."

"Right. They had to replace several parts to allow it to carry more weight." Margie shook her head. "I'm not even going to try to interpret all of the stuff in here about rotor speed and battery life and what individual parts were modified."

"Uh-huh."

"But there were a lot more modifications than that. And they are still puzzling over some of the parts that were swapped in and what they can learn from them all."

"Give a modified drone to the tech geeks, and what do you expect? They'll probably take longer to issue their report than the ME will to issue his."

Margie chuckled and agreed. She continued to make her way through the report. "Apparently, a drone that large has to be registered with Transport Canada. So they can search by serial number to see who the owner was."

Cruz looked away from the road for a moment and raised his brows. "So we know where it came from! Is there any chance Xander Cartier was the registered owner? I don't imagine those things come cheap, and he definitely comes from money."

"The outside serial number was ground off. But it is also imprinted inside. They have traced it back to a Grant Paxton." Margie read through the following lines. "So we might have our drone pilot."

"Excellent. We can find out whether he works at the same place as Xander and whether he was a known associate."

Margie let out a sigh of relief. It was a big break. Did the pilot really think that removing the serial number would be enough to obscure the ownership of the drone? Did he think that would make him anonymous?

They had him. And if he had been the one to kill Xander Cartier, they would get him for that too.

"That's good news," she agreed.

CHAPTER TWELVE

*C*ruz pulled over to the curb and Margie looked up from her phone to have a look at the house. She had expected it to be a big, fancy house, and was not disappointed.

The house's footprint was probably four times the size of Margie's little bungalow, and it rose two to three stories, depending on which part of the house she was looking at. At the corners were turrets reminiscent of a castle. In the front, a multipaned window rose to the full two stories of the living room or great room and was at least as wide as Margie's house. Such large windows would mean huge electric bills for AC during the summer and natural gas during the winter. They were beautiful, not practical. Although they would provide a lot of light on a sunny day.

They didn't get out of the car. No point in standing on the front step until Mr. Cartier opened the front door as promised. They would just get tired standing around and might as well take the opportunity to sit in the car and chat and review any other emailed reports or do whatever else they could on their mobile devices. Margie couldn't do all of the background checks on her phone, but she could certainly troll social media posts and see whether Xander had any obvious connection with Grant Paxton.

Grant Paxton was easy to find on social media. He was clearly an airplane enthusiast. Selfies showed him at various airports and air shows, and his feeds were full of airplane museums, airplanes in flight, Paxton at the controls of a private plane, and more than one picture of him operating a drone or showing off the footage he had taken from a drone.

"Wow, this guy is really into planes."

"Who, Xander?"

"Paxton. Like, multiple pictures each day. He must be retired, because it looks like all he does is go from one plane spotting location to another. He flies himself, as well as piloting drones. And I don't think it is the same drone in each picture. He must have a few of them."

"A few of them?" Cruz repeated. "Don't these things run to the tens of thousands?"

"And at least one full-sized plane." Margie swiped through pictures. "No, make that two."

"So financially, he's on par with Cartier. Are they connected?"

"Neither has an open friends list, so I'm not sure. I'll check their wives. Women have accessible friends lists more often than men."

"That's a rather biased viewpoint," Cruz teased.

"Do you share your friends list?"

"No, of course not."

"Does your wife?"

Cruz looked at her sideways. "Shut up."

Margie laughed. She found the wives' profiles and browsed through their friends lists. She didn't find any overlaps between them. Not only were they not friends, but they appeared to run in entirely different circles.

"Both wealthy, but no connections I can see. It must be between Xander and Paxton. Or maybe Xander just happened to be in the park and saw something by accident."

Cruz nodded. He pulled out his notepad and jotted down a few notes.

"Anything you want to share?" Margie asked, since he didn't comment about what he was writing down. Was he just noting the tidbits she had told him, or writing down his own conclusions and investigative path?

"Nothing to share yet," Cruz said with a shrug, putting it back away.

"Where do you think this case is going to break? Investigating the drone or Xander Cartier's murder?"

"Don't know yet. Finding out who owned the drone is a big step. That may be all that it takes."

Margie nodded. Unlike Hollywood, in real life the guilty person tended to be just who you figured it would be. There were exceptions, of course, but it held true that most women were killed by their spouses; children were kidnapped by their parents, friends, or close relations; and most criminals were average to low average intelligence, not the brilliant evil masterminds of TV.

"There he is," Cruz said, unbuckling his seatbelt. Margie looked at the front door and saw that it had been opened. Mr. Cartier hovered in the doorway until they got out of the car, then retreated to be with his wife rather than waiting for them to walk up the sidewalk. Cruz and Margie stepped into the house and could immediately see the couple sitting on a cream-colored couch in the airy great room. Mr. Cartier had his arm around his wife, who was sobbing into his shoulder. Mr. Cartier himself still looked stunned and was not crying. He probably wouldn't until they were gone. Maybe not until after his son was buried and everyone else went on with their lives. Margie had seen men with his type A personality implode. They kept going, denying their own feelings, until they could go no further.

"Mr. Cartier, Mrs. Cartier, I'm very sorry for your loss," Margie said, knowing that her repeated expressions of sympathy meant little to them. She was there to probe their wounds in the hopes of finding some piece of information that would help them find the person who had killed Xander.

Margie sat down on a Queen Anne chair, leaning slightly forward.

"I know that you are not ready for questions right now. But I'm wondering if you can tell me where Xander worked."

Mrs. Cartier sobbed and pulled her face away from her husband's body. Tears leaked from the corners of her eyes, and she blinked at Margie as if unable to see her through the stormy weather.

She had curly red hair—a dye job, Margie thought, but a good one. Her makeup, probably perfect before her husband had returned home to give her the terrible news, was now smudged and running together. She pulled a tissue from a box on the side table and dabbed at her eyes, trying to wipe the tears and makeup away, making a distressed mew when she realized her face was a mess.

"It's fine," Mr. Cartier told her, pulling a couple more tissues out and wiping her face gently, looking down into her anguished expression. "You look fine. Don't worry about that."

She nodded and tried to speak to Margie, her voice hoarse and nose clogged.

"He worked at Ferguson Miller Tech. He is—was—a computer programmer and IT support. Kept their systems running. Sometimes he was there late at night, getting everything straightened out long after everyone else had left. I told him he shouldn't be staying there all by himself. It wasn't safe."

Margie nodded her understanding. She wrote down the name of the company.

"He wasn't killed in the office," Mr. Cartier informed his wife. "It wasn't anything to do with his work."

Neither of the detectives corrected him to say they didn't know whether it had anything to do with his work. He hadn't been at the office, but that didn't mean it wasn't work-related. Sometimes, issues that began at work spilled out of the office. Jealousies, resentments, and romances didn't necessarily stay at work.

"He was at Prairie Winds Park," Margie told Mrs. Cartier. "Do you know where that is?"

"Miles said he was at the airport."

Margie glanced at Mr. Cartier, who responded with a slight shake of his head. "*Near* the airport," he corrected. "In a park near the airport."

"But why would he be there? In the middle of the day? He should have been at work."

"We don't know for sure. Did he ever mention that park to you? It wasn't a place that you used to take him?" Margie probed.

"No. Why would I take him there?"

"Sledding as a kid. The wading pool or splash park. It's a fun place for kids."

Mrs. Cartier stared at her. Margie shrugged.

"I just wondered whether it was a place he was familiar with from childhood. If not, we know he didn't just go out there to reminisce about good times. He didn't mention it to you? Was it close to his work?"

"No. Not if it was near the airport."

"Do you know if he was having any trouble at work?"

"Trouble at work? I thought this was just a random thing. What do you mean?"

"We don't know yet what happened. We are still investigating. We don't know if it was related to work, to something to do with this drone, or just a chance thing, being in the wrong place at the wrong time. I wish we had more answers right now. Anything you could provide would be helpful."

"He didn't talk about work. Not very much. Neither of us understood much of what he did there. He could try to explain it, and we would nod and act interested... but the technical stuff just went over my head." She glanced at her husband. "Maybe you understood some of it."

"No, dear." He touched her cheek and used his thumb to wipe away a fresh tear. "I had no clue."

She gave a little gasp of a laugh at that. "We are two old fogies. Even my mother knows more about computers than I do. She's a whiz on the phone, and she can find anything on the internet. She was the one teaching us how to do Zoom during the COVID lockdown."

"Was Xander having any problems in other parts of his life? Relationship issues? An ongoing argument with a neighbor? Did he have any habits that worried you?" Cruz suggested.

"Habits?" Mrs. Cartier shook her head, not understanding.

"Sometimes young people get into gambling or using substances without realizing what problems it may cause them."

"No, no. Nothing like that. Xander was a good boy. He wasn't into any of that kind of thing. He didn't even like to go to bars with his friends. Said there were more productive ways to use his time."

"Did you have concerns about anything? Anyone in his life?"

Both parents shook their heads. Many parents would have said the same thing. They often didn't know what was happening in their children's lives or didn't want to see the problem areas. It was common to be in denial after a sudden death.

Margie nodded. "Okay. I'm going to leave you alone now. I'm sorry for having to disturb you. Is there any way we can help you? Someone you would like us to call or questions you want to ask?" she reached into her pocket and took out a business card. "I'm going to leave you with my number, so if something comes up later, you can reach me."

"Just… what do we do about arrangements…?" Mrs. Cartier sniffled. "I've never had to deal with something like this before."

"If you have a particular funeral home in mind, you can just have them call the Office of the Chief Medical Examiner, and they will make arrangements to transfer your son's remains once the medical examiner is finished. If you don't have someone in mind yet, that's fine. Take your time. Call me or the medical examiner when you are ready. You don't have to go in to identify him."

"Okay. Thank you. I'll… I guess we will be in touch. Will you… let us know when you know something?"

"Of course. We will let you know if an arrest is made. Someone will probably be by Xander's house today to see if there is anything that might be connected to his death there."

They nodded.

Margie left her card on the coffee table and stood up. She didn't shake hands with either of them. She and Cruz nodded respectfully to the couple and then let themselves out.

CHAPTER THIRTEEN

*W*hen they sat down in the car, Cruz looked up the address for Ferguson Miller Tech. "You want to pass that information on to the team? They can start looking into the company and if they were in any trouble."

"Sure," Margie agreed and quickly tapped out a message to the rest of the team. "Do you think they had anything to do with the drone?"

"You can see if you can find a connection between Paxton and Ferguson Miller before we get there. The parents didn't make any automatic connection between drones and the company, so I suspect not. If the kid was working on drone technology and then was killed watching a drone launch, that would have raised suspicions."

Margie started searching as soon as she had sent the update email out, combining the names and searching them in various search engines and social networks. Nothing popped up.

When she looked up to see where they were, they were in an area completely unfamiliar to Margie. Cruz had not bothered to type the address into his GPS app. In a few minutes, they pulled in front of a low building in the light industrial area. There were numbers on the doors, but no big signs or awnings with the names of the companies on them. Cruz and Margie walked up to the door and saw Ferguson Miller Tech stenciled on it in small letters. They entered and a door-bell chime announced their entry as they crossed an invisible barrier.

A man in a t-shirt came out to the front counter where Margie and Cruz stood.

"Yeah, can I help you?"

"We are looking for Xander Cartier's boss," Cruz informed him.

"What about?"

"We will discuss that with him."

"Well, that would be me. So what is it?"

"Was Xander scheduled to work today?" Margie asked curiously.

"Yes, he was supposed to be here this morning. Don't know what happened to him. He hasn't answered his phone or texts. Who are you and why are you asking?"

"Is there somewhere private we could meet?" Cruz suggested.

"Do you see anyone else around?" The man made a motion to indicate the reception area, which, of course, was empty.

"Detectives Cruz and Patenaude from the Calgary Police," Cruz said. "I regret to inform you that Mr. Cartier was killed yesterday."

"Killed?" The brusque manager was taken aback by this information. "What do you mean, killed? Like he was hit by a bus or something?"

"By a bullet," Cruz said baldly.

The man's jaw dropped open. "You're kidding." His eyes darted around, and he shook his head. "Is this some kind of prank? It isn't very funny. Do you have identification of some kind? Is this...? Do you have hidden cameras?"

"No. This is not a joke or prank. We are serious." Cruz pulled out his identification, and Margie followed his example, presenting hers.

The man stared at them and shook his head slowly. "Killed? Murdered? I never would have expected that in a million years. Xander was steady. Cool-headed. I wouldn't expect him to get in the way of a bullet."

"Could we sit down somewhere to meet?" Cruz suggested.

The man who said he was Xander's boss nodded, his eyes wide.

"Yes, of course... I don't know what I can tell you, but..."

He motioned them around the counter and into the workspace that contained the actual operations of Ferguson Miller Tech. There were lots of computers and monitors, and a variety of equipment Margie couldn't identify. It was mostly an open layout, with workbenches and computer desks that gave Margie a feeling similar to the bullpen she worked in. A few people were at work, mostly dressed as Xander had been, in casual collared shirts and khakis. They didn't have lanyards with name badges; it was a small office where everyone knew everyone else.

Several sets of eyes watched the boss escort Margie and Cruz to a walled-off meeting room that would give them some privacy. There was a layer of dust over everything. It was obviously not used or cleaned very often. The man shut the door and motioned for them to sit at the table. A far cry from the meeting room where they had met with Xander's father not long ago.

"Uh, my name is Carey Stepaniak. Sorry, I don't think I

introduced myself." He sat down at the table and wrung his hands, appearing at a loss about what he should do or say.

"Good to meet you, Mr. Stepaniak," Margie tried to keep her voice calm and reassuring. "This is Detective Cruz, and I am Detective Patenaude. Some people prefer Detective Pat; it is easier to remember."

"Oh, you don't need to tell me about difficult last names," he gave a little laugh, "You wouldn't believe some of the things I get called. I just go by Carey here, so why don't you stick to that."

Margie nodded. "Of course, Carey," she agreed, using it immediately to put him at ease. "I'm sorry to have to talk to you about Xander when I am sure you can hardly wrap your mind around the idea of him being dead. But we are in the middle of an investigation, and anything you can help us with is appreciated."

"Yeah, of course. I don't think there is anything I can do, but I'll try."

"How long had he been working here?"

"Just for a few months. I had another employee who resigned without notice and left us in the lurch here, so Xander is the newbie. We had to bring someone in from outside with the skills needed to take over on the project. Unfortunately, there aren't many people with Xander's type of experience. There weren't a lot of candidates who could step in and fill the position."

"I understand he was a computer programmer and IT support?"

Carey made a motion that indicated the workspace outside the meeting room. "You can see that we are into computer technologies. It's hard to explain to people exactly what it is that we do. We are... developing the technologies that are embedded in everyday household appliances. Look at a washing machine on the market today and compare it to what you might have purchased fifteen years ago. There is no comparison. Today's appliances connect to your home Wi-Fi. They are programmable. They weigh and analyze your load to determine how much water to use, what temperature, how long the cycles are, and so on."

"And you work on the electronics that do that?"

"Yeah. Our electronics can be found in washers, cars, automated vacuum cleaners, fridges, all that sort of thing. Blenders and food processors. Microwaves. Anything in your house that you can program or talk to."

"So it's really sophisticated stuff."

"It is," Carey agreed. "We need highly skilled people. I was glad to find Xander. He was a good addition to the team. Until…"

He didn't finish the sentence, and Margie wasn't sure if he meant until now, when he had been taken from them so abruptly, or if he was talking about something else.

"Was everything okay with his performance?" she nudged. "Did he get along with people?"

"Geeks aren't always the best at socialization," Carey said with a laugh. "We have some… difficult personalities here. Xander didn't cause any problems. We might have had differences of opinion, but he had the skills he needed, and he managed to work with this ragtag bunch pretty well."

"Then you didn't have any concerns?"

There was a slight hesitation before Carey answered. A flicker of something, Margie wasn't sure what.

"No concerns," he said. "You weren't… expecting anything, were you?"

"Did you know if he had any issues with his personal life? Or were there any resentments about him coming in on this project like he did? Maybe somebody else thought that they should have been offered the job? Or didn't like him for some reason?"

"No. Xander was a good kid. I don't think anyone had any problems with him. He wasn't... he wasn't killed here. You don't think this had anything to do with his work, do you?" Carey shook his head. "No one here would have done anything to harm him."

Cruz and Margie both smiled reassuringly.

"I'm sure it wasn't anything to do with work. We just need to follow up on all the possibilities," Margie told him.

"Okay. Well, no, I don't know of anyone who had any reason to be resentful or jealous of him. Everybody seemed pretty good about Xander coming on board. And no, I don't know of any personal or family problems. I don't think he had a girlfriend and he wasn't the type to go out to the bar or to gamble or anything like that. I can't think of any trouble he might have gotten himself into. It must have been... just a random thing. Just being in the wrong place at the wrong time?"

"It's possible," Margie agreed. She looked out at the work floor through the narrow window beside the door. "What about drones? Do you have anything to do with them?"

"Err... drones?"

"With your computer programming, do you have any projects that involve drones? You said you have your technology in cars; what about drones?"

He shook his head slowly. "We don't have anything like that on the market. I wouldn't rule it out. You could certainly use our technology in an application like that. If there was enough demand."

Margie nodded. "Was Xander into drones, do you know? As a hobbyist?"

"No, I wouldn't know anything about that. I don't know what he did in his free time. He spent a lot of long hours here, I have to admit. We tend to get wrapped up in things... you don't like to leave when you have one more thing to try…" He shrugged. "There is always one more little glitch to get fixed. You do that, and something else pops up. You think it will just take five minutes, and two hours later, you're still struggling with it."

"His parents said that he was often here alone. They worried about him being out here by himself."

"I don't know if that is true. I have to admit that we are not strict about what hours people work. If you want to work until two in the morning and don't come in until noon the next day, that's really not a problem. Employees track their time so that we can make sure they are putting in the hours, but that is more something we have to do for government reporting than because we are concerned about people not putting in enough time."

He scratched his head and thought about it.

"Xander was usually here during the day when I was around. I'd have to check his timesheets and compare them to everyone else's to see if he was spending a lot of time alone here by himself. But I don't see why that would be a problem. You know, some people just work best at night or when things are quiet."

"What projects was he working on? What kind of technologies?"

"That's highly confidential. We don't talk about our products before they are released. There is a lot of corporate espionage, you know. We have to make sure that doesn't leak out."

"Maybe you could just tell us in general terms what sorts of projects he was working on."

"I've already done that," Carey pointed out.

"Vacuums, cars, blenders? You can't tell us anything more specific?"

"I really don't see why I need to. It doesn't have anything

to do with Xander's death. He didn't die here, or because of something he was doing here."

Margie couldn't prove that he had. There was no evidence to suggest that it had something to do with work, so she didn't press.

"Well... thank you for your time. I appreciate it. If you think of anything that may be significant, please give me a call." Margie handed him one of her cards. "Do you happen to know a Grant Paxton?"

Carey frowned. "No, I don't think so. Should I?"

"Just someone that Xander knew."

"No, I don't think I ever heard him mention that name."

Margie nodded. "Okay, thanks. If anyone says anything... sometimes when someone has died, people start to talk about them, and if things come up that we should know about... you hear of any conflicts he had or just anything that makes you wonder... drop me a line or give me a call."

"Sure, yeah." Carey stood up. He offered his hand. "Thanks for coming by."

Margie shook his hand, and she and Cruz went back to the car.

CHAPTER FOURTEEN

Cruz pulled out his phone after sitting down.

"MacDonald says since we're already halfway there, can we go out to talk to Paxton."

Margie's heart sped when she thought about seeing the drone owner and suspected murderer. It was always anxiety-producing to confront someone who looked good for a violent crime. She knew it was essential to use that adrenaline to stay sharp and think ahead as they confronted him. Not to let it make her sloppy or hesitant.

"Yeah, of course," she agreed.

Maybe they would get him today. It was always nice when they could put a murderer behind bars within days, rather than taking months to gather enough evidence to arrest him.

Cruz nodded. He shot a text back to MacDonald and buckled his seatbelt.

"You know where it is?" Margie asked.

He grinned at her. "Do you even have to ask?"

"I don't know how you learned the city so well."

"And he's outside the city. Out where he can fly his planes."

"Oh. Of course."

"I had a friend out that way, so I know where it is," Cruz said with an easy shrug.

They took an eastbound road out of town. Margie watched out the window as they got farther away from the mountains. The ground got flatter and there were fewer trees. The fields were not yet green or gold with crops. It was still too early in the year to plant safely, even though the temperatures had been good lately.

"Do we know anything about him yet?" she asked Cruz, unsure how much information he had gotten from MacDonald when he asked if they would go interview him.

"All I know is what you pulled up on his social media. That he's an aviation nut. If he had a criminal record, we would have been told that. But I guess they didn't find anything concerning."

Margie nodded. "Good." She pulled up his feed on her phone again and looked through the various posts. There wasn't anything that suggested to her that he might be the least bit violent. A lot of stuff on planes, some on his family, but nothing about guns or being upset about any particular person or cause. "Yeah, he checks out fine on social media. Doesn't go off on rants about anything."

"Good," Cruz nodded. "Always best to know if you are going up against a gun nut or someone who constantly posts about how he hates cops."

"Exactly."

Margie closed her eyes to rest them while they traveled to the Paxton farm. Despite the adrenaline rush of going to see a potential murderer, she was feeling her lack of sleep the night before. A few minutes with her eyes closed would help to clear her head.

It felt like she had barely closed them when Cruz announced, "We're here," and turned onto a gravel road.

Margie straightened up and rubbed her eyes, unsure whether she had drifted off for a few minutes or if they had just been that close to the farm when she had closed her eyes.

"You okay?" Cruz asked. "You need a minute?"

"No, I'm good." Margie swigged a little cold coffee, wincing at the bitterness, and looked around.

It wasn't much to look at. If Paxton was as wealthy as Xander's father, the place sure didn't look like it. A little farmhouse with an add-on enclosed porch. Several cars in the driveway. Some metal prefab outbuildings. Overgrown grass and trees near the farmhouse. Wide open land beyond the outbuildings. She assumed the buildings housed the airplanes and drones, along with whatever farm equipment Paxton might use for his gentleman-farmer chores. She doubted he kept animals or planted crops—there had been no sign of that on his social media.

Dogs barked as they pulled off of the gravel road into the driveway and approached the house. Margie looked at Cruz, and they waited. It was common courtesy for the property owner to come to the door to see who his dogs were barking at, and to call them off if it were someone he consented to see. A couple of minutes passed before a man appeared at the door of the house. He called off the dogs, telling them to shut up and lie down. They returned to the shelter of the porch and lay down quietly there.

"Who are you?" Paxton asked Margie and Cruz. "You lost?"

Margie rolled her window down and held her badge up for him to see. "Calgary Police, Mr. Paxton."

"Police?" He ran his fingers through his thinning hair. "What do you want?"

"Can we come in for a chat?"

"Sure."

He held the door open for them, and they all walked into the house and sat in the dimly lit living room. There were no lights on, and the windows were screened by trees. That probably kept it cool in the heat of the summer, but it made it seem dark and dingy on a spring afternoon after coming in from the bright, fresh sunshine.

"What's this all about?"

"You registered a drone with Transport Canada," Cruz started.

"Sure, I've got a couple," Paxton agreed, a grin splitting his face. "I love flying."

"Have you got the description and serial number there?" Cruz asked Margie. She pulled out her phone and navigated to the report she had been looking at earlier. She recited the model and serial number. Paxton shook his head.

"Nope. Sold that one."

"You sold it? To who?"

"A young guy. Just getting started with drones, didn't know much about them yet. Xander Cartier."

Margie and Cruz exchanged looks.

"Xander Cartier," Cruz repeated.

"Yeah, kind of a weird name, and it stuck in my mind. I guess his family has a ton of money, and he decided to get into drones."

"The drone is registered with Transport Canada in your name."

"Yeah, because it used to be mine. I told him he would have to reregister it. I thought he understood. I gave him all of the paperwork." He shrugged. "Kids these days. They tend to be kind of lazy. I guess he got into testing it out and never got around to registering it. What happened? Don't tell me he crashed it."

"What did you know about him? Did he find you, or did you have mutual friends?" Margie asked.

"I don't know anything about him except that he wanted to learn to fly drones and had the cash to do it. He knew the specs he had worked out that he needed, and I had what he was looking for."

"Why were you getting rid of it? I thought flying was your thing."

"It is," Paxton agreed, smiling again. He leaned forward to talk to them. "You know how some people are always early adopters of the new iPhone or whatever the next big thing is? They'll put down fifteen hundred or two thousand dollars on the new release, even though they know it will go down in a few months. And then there are the people who wait until a phone is five or six years old before they get it. They wait until it is almost obsolete, and they can get it for two or three hundred."

Margie nodded her understanding. "And you are an early adopter."

"I have to have the next big thing in drones. I'll get it at ten or twenty thousand, and in three years, sell it for two or three. Yeah, I spend a lot of money that way, but what else is it for? It's to bring me joy, right? Drones and planes make me happy, so that's what I spend it on. And then I make someone who can't afford to buy it new happy." He grinned like a kid.

"And Xander bought it from you used so that he could get a good deal. Get started with something cheap and see how it worked for him."

Paxton nodded. "That's right. He seemed real eager to get it. Like I said, he knew the specs and what he wanted. Didn't dicker with the price. Paid his money and took it home with him."

Margie frowned at this. Xander lived in the city. Where was he going to store or fly a drone? It wasn't like it was one of the ones that kids or photographers used. It was big enough to carry a payload of 150 pounds. Or it was once it had been modified. It was big.

She looked at Cruz, shaking her head. He seemed to understand.

"How did he pay you?" Cruz asked. "Was it cash up front?"

"E-transfer. So much better than checks and money orders!"

"He e-transferred you while he was here? So you had it in hand and he could walk away with the merchandise. You knew you had been paid in full."

"Yeah. No risk. So much nicer. I signed over ownership to Xander and he took it with him. He had a truck and I helped him load it up. Gave him plenty of advice," Paxton's weathered cheeks turned a little pink at that comment. "Probably way more than he wanted to hear. But I didn't want him making any big mistakes. It's not like flying a kite."

"No, they can be dangerous," Cruz agreed.

"So what did he do?" Paxton persisted. "Did he crash it? I hope to heaven no one was hurt."

Margie sighed. "Did you see the news about the drone that entered the YYC airspace?"

"What?" Paxton demanded. He nearly jumped out of his chair in his agitation. "Tell me that wasn't him!" He swore. "He knew better than to do something like that! Flying it into the airport? What was he thinking?"

"That's what we're trying to figure out." Margie considered how much to tell him. If he was telling the truth about having sold it to Xander, and since he had offered Xander's name, she believed it to be true, he was not the murderer.

Why would he sell it to Xander and then hunt him down at Prairie Winds Park and shoot him?

Of course, there was the possibility that he could have. There could have been some kind of tracking chip on the drone that would allow him to see its location, track it down, and confront Xander about what he was doing. But why would he do that?

"Who modified the drone?" Cruz asked. "Was that you or Xander?"

"I don't do a lot of modding. Not like a lot of guys. I'd replaced some parts on it. Gave it a better battery so that I could fly it for longer. But nothing extreme. What had been modified?"

Cruz looked at Margie, since she was the one who had been reading about what the technicians had been able to figure out overnight.

"Well, it was modified to carry a bigger payload," Margie said, looking down at the long, technical explanation on the report and trying to condense it. "I guess that meant a bigger motor and rotors."

"Bigger payload? What was he doing with it? It was designed to carry camera equipment. You want to stay light and agile if you use it for video recording."

"We think he was going to use it to take something into the airport. Can you think of why he would want to do that?"

"What, like explosives? *My* drone?" Paxton sounded outraged at the thought that someone would buy a drone from him and use it for nefarious purposes. "No way!"

"We don't know if that was his plan. It looks like yesterday's flight was intended to be reconnaissance. And then he would go back in later with... whatever he planned to transport inside the fence."

"That's why he—" Paxton started, then cut himself off.

Margie and Cruz both waited. He had something to spill, they could tell. Paxton's eyes were big, and he looked like he would have shot Xander himself if the younger man had been there.

"I wouldn't sell it to a terrorist," Paxton insisted. "He didn't look like a terrorist. He was Canadian. White. He didn't look… like one of *them*."

"You can't always tell what someone has in their heart," Margie said. "White people have been radicalized. Women, teenagers. You don't know."

"He said he wanted to take up flying drones as a hobby. He had the money and it seemed like a fun thing to do. How was I supposed to know he was planning an attack?"

"I don't know how you could have," Margie assured him. "But you started to say something a minute ago. What was it? That was why he… what? Why he modified it? Why he was looking for the specs that he was? What were you about to say?"

Paxton rubbed the bridge of his nose. He shook his head and swore.

"He looked like a good kid. Just like the other kids I fly with sometimes. They're so eager to get into it. He looked geeky, excited about playing around with the planes. Like the little RC cars they got when they were six, or little helicopters that would fly for about thirty seconds before they crashed. Just a clean-cut young man with his head on straight."

Margie thought about how Xander had looked to her. A young professional. Geeky, like Paxton said. The furthest thing from a terrorist.

"I don't think you did anything wrong. I don't think you could have known Xander planned to do anything wrong. It isn't like he would have told you."

"You don't have to do a background check before you sell a drone to someone. I've never done that before. I've sold drones ten times and never had problems with anyone."

"That was why…" Margie prompted again.

Paxton looked miserable.

"That was why he bought two."

CHAPTER FIFTEEN

Margie's heart skipped a beat. She felt nauseated. She looked at Cruz, and while his expression was carefully masked, she knew he felt exactly the same way.

They had thought that it was over, or they at least had time before another attempt could be made. Xander or the terrorist group had failed at their plan when the RCMP had managed to jam the control signal and bring the drone down. They figured that whatever the intent had been, those who had planned the incursion had failed. They would need to get another drone and start over.

But Paxton knew the truth. Xander or the mastermind of the attack had known that the reconnaissance drone would be captured. They had known that from the start. The test drone would be captured, but if they had succeeded in gathering the information they needed for the actual mission, they would now be able to proceed with the second drone to deliver whatever payload they had planned.

Margie shook her head. "We'd better make some calls."

❧

SHE AND CRUZ spitballed ideas as they drove back to the office. They had broken the news to MacDonald that there was already a second drone prepared, and when they got back to the office, they hoped to have some kind of handle on what was happening.

"Xander didn't shoot himself," Margie said, "and he didn't have the drone controller on him when we found him. So we know he was working with someone. Someone out there knows exactly what he was up to. They have the information that the first drone collected on its reconnaissance trip, and they have the second drone ready, so they can send it in with... whatever the payload is."

"Was this Xander's idea?" Cruz asked. "Was he a terrorist? Or is this something else?"

"Whatever it is, he knew it was illegal. He knew that the first drone would be captured. They probably know a lot more about airport security than we gave them credit for. They didn't naively think they would be able to get the drone out and then send it back a second time for the real op."

"His parents didn't know anything about it," Cruz said. "His boss didn't know anything about it. Nor did Paxton. So *who* was he working with?"

Margie fired back suggestions as quickly as she could think of them. "A girlfriend."

Girlfriends were great at convincing guys to do things they wouldn't normally do.

"Parents and boss both say he didn't have one."

"Someone he worked with."

"Boss would have known something was going on between them."

"Someone he played games with online."

"Maybe," Cruz allowed, considering it. "Xander's parents

thought he was working nights. Maybe he was gaming and didn't want them to know about it."

"And his gaming partner wanted to take it to real life. Stop flying simulations and fly a drone. Stop doing covert missions in the game world and do it in real life. Start having some real-life experiences. They might have worked up to it, challenging each other to try different things in real life. It could be a terrorist disguising himself as another geek Xander's age who shared his interests. But then Xander balked or changed his mind. He'd gone as far as he dared and grew a conscience. The so-called friend takes him out so that Xander can't spill what he already knows or point the finger at him."

"Interesting idea," Cruz complimented. "And when I go home today, I'm going to ban all the kids from online gaming."

Margie grinned. "Good luck with that. They'll just go to other people's houses to play. Or go 'study' at the library."

THERE WAS SO much information coming in so fast on the case that Margie had a hard time processing all of the files and getting up to speed on the other leads that had been investigated while they were away from the office.

It was one case rather than two, now that Paxton had conclusively linked the drone and Xander.

Siever hovered over Margie's shoulder as she tried to skim through all the files so she would at least know what they were all about, even if she didn't have time to read them all.

"Can we meet?" he asked impatiently.

Margie stared at the screen. "I don't know if we have time before the briefing. I was hoping to get up to speed on this."

"I'm supposed to be presenting in the briefing. I need to

explain the modifications to the drone so that everyone can understand them."

Margie leaned back in her chair and rubbed her palms over her eyes, wishing there were time for a nap or a shower. "Okay," she agreed. "We can go through it."

"I'll get you coffee."

"Yeah, I'm gonna need it. Especially if we're talking about technology."

"I'll meet you in conference room B. Go splash water on your face."

Margie nodded. "Okay. I'll be there in a minute."

Siever was straightforward to the point of being blunt, but Margie didn't mind that. It was just the way he communicated. He was the best guy to have on hand when they needed any kind of technical analysis. He understood how technology fit into their investigations and was able to compile data and present it to the rest of the team in a way they could understand.

But meetings, even their regular briefings, made him nervous. He worried about presenting to everyone and was easily flustered or thrown off his stride with questions. Margie would do her best to help him organize his thoughts so he would be ready.

Splashing cold water on her face helped to chase the cobwebs away, and together with the caffeine, would have to stand in for a nap. She sat down with Siever in the meeting room.

"Okay, tell me what you've got."

"There's too much to cover everything."

"There always is. We already know it was modified for a heavier payload, so you don't need to include that."

Siever nodded. "Right."

"What was the next biggest modification?"

He tapped the keys of his laptop lightly without pressing any of them. "There was a lot."

"One thing at a time."

"They installed a Raspberry Pi."

Margie gazed at him. "I'm sure that means something different from what it sounds like."

He gave a brief smile at that. "It's not actual pie."

"I didn't think so. Though pie sounds like an excellent idea right now."

"Raspberry Pi is… it's like a miniaturized computer."

"Okay," Margie nodded. "I can understand that. How is that different from the computer that was already on it?"

"Did you read the report from this morning? The tech department's findings so far?"

"Yes. It kind of blew my mind. I didn't know drones were that sophisticated. I thought the rotors lifted it in the air, and the controller determined which direction it went, and that was all there was to it. But from what I read, it does all kinds of calculations to help it stay level and handle any weather conditions or smooth out directional commands from the controller."

"Right."

"So that's the onboard computer it comes with? That's what it does out of the box?"

"Sort of. Those flight algorithms are on a chip. It's not a full-blown computer."

"And this Strawberry Pi…"

"Raspberry," he corrected. "Raspberry Pi *is* a computer. So you can program it to do a lot more things that the drone can't do out of the box. You can make it do anything, really. It could… track license plates, Wi-Fi signals, do facial recognition… it could gather all kinds of data about its surroundings, not just save a video recording or send it back to the pilot. It could send signals and receive them. It could be programmed with whatever you can think of."

"That's terrifying."

Siever looked at her and nodded.

"Okay." Margie considered this. "Do we know what it was programmed to do?"

"The techs are seeing what they can do to figure it out. But it's not as easy as just reading lines of code. It has layers of protection."

"So we need to be ready for anything. Consider this drone—the second drone that is coming—to be highly sophisticated and capable of doing anything we can think of. Is there any way to tell if they are weaponizing it? This one just had ballast. What if the second one has explosives or ammunition?"

"Whoever made the plan obviously didn't want us to know or be prepared for what the second drone would be carrying," Siever confirmed.

"Yeah."

"There is a good amount of data saved on the recovered drone. We don't know what it all might be. Not yet."

"And we don't know when the second drone is coming."

"It could be today. It could be a year from now when no one is expecting it. And it could be a different airport in a different city."

"Unless we can physically track the second drone," Margie suggested. "Find out where it is being stored."

"They executed a warrant on Xander's house today. It's not there. There isn't any sign that they were ever there."

"There is at least one other person mixed up in this. We don't know who it is, but someone killed Xander. Someone else is storing that drone. And planning to fly it. Whatever Xander decided he didn't want to be a part of, someone else is still planning to put into action."

Siever nodded.

"Any other surprises?" Margie asked. "A self-destruct button?"

He shrugged. "It could have any kind of self-destruct or data wiping protocol."

THEY GOT down a few bullet points for Siever to relay at the briefing meeting, keeping it as short as possible, and promising to follow up on any questions later. Siever was much calmer once they'd had a chance to go over the information.

"You're getting to be old hat at this," Margie told him. "One day, you'll just walk in there and give your report without any special prep."

He rolled his eyes and shook his head. "I don't think so."

"We'll see. You are getting better all the time."

He smiled his appreciation, but didn't agree.

Margie and Cruz reported on their visits to Ferguson Miller and Paxton's farm. Everyone had already heard the news of the second drone, and the anxiety in the room over what Xander's mysterious partner planned to do with it was palpable.

"Do we think Xander was radicalized?" Jones asked. "Do we think he had contact with terrorists and was trained by them? I've looked through everything we have on his history and background, and I can't find anything that makes sense. He did well in school. He wasn't unpopular. He came from a wealthy family, but it doesn't seem like they spoiled him. There's no reason for him to be disaffected. And there isn't anything in his social networks that suggests he was."

They looked around the room at each other, but no one could come up with anything. Margie floated the theory that it might have been an online friend and that Xander had eventually backed out of whatever they had planned when he realized what they were really up to. It wasn't anything that anyone could disprove or that they could prove. It was all theoretical. But it fit.

"Without his partner's background, it is impossible to know what they were planning, what that drone was programmed to do," Jones pointed out. "We only have half of the equation. Maybe not even half."

MacDonald made additional assignments and looked at his watch. "Everyone has already put in a lot of hours," he said. "We don't know when things are going to happen on this file, or even if the partner still intends to proceed. You can't run on empty, so you need to go home and get some sleep tonight. We will have plenty of work to do tomorrow. The computer guys will continue to work on the data on the drone and where it might point. Rest tonight so you will be fresh in the morning."

It was a letdown. They had been hoping to have made a lot more progress by the end of the day. It was discouraging to realize that there was another drone out there, and they had no idea what its instructions or abilities were or who else was involved in the operation.

But MacDonald was right. They couldn't run on empty. Tomorrow would be another day.

CHAPTER SIXTEEN

*C*hristina was home when Margie got there, but glancing around, Margie didn't think she had been there for long. Her school bag had been dumped near the front door, where she usually left it when she arrived home and had to take Stella out immediately. There were no food smells and only the main living room and kitchen lights were turned on.

"Hi, sweetie," Margie greeted, giving her a quick hug after dealing with Stella's demands for affection. "How was your day today? Were you out with Tracy?"

"Yeah. We had supper with his family and did homework over there."

"That's nice. How is Tracy doing?"

"Good. He just got word that he got a scholarship that he applied for." Christina's forehead wrinkled. "I guess I should be applying for scholarships."

Margie wished she had savings set aside for Christina's education, but unfortunately, she didn't. Working as a law enforcement officer in Winnipeg while paying for childcare had not brought in much money. They had been living lean for years, getting by but not able to put much away. Margie contributed to an RRSP and had a little bit of money in the bank for emergencies or unexpected expenses, but U of C cost thousands of dollars per semester, and even the smaller colleges and technical schools could be pricey. Christina would take a summer job to help pay for it, and Margie might need to do something on the side as well. A scholarship or two would go a long way to making it easier.

"Your guidance counselor at school should be able to help you find scholarships you qualify for. There are some for Métis students, girls who want to go into science, I don't know what else. And depending on your marks in your final year of high school, there are some others you may qualify for as well."

Christina pushed her hair back over her ear. "Okay. I guess I'll set up an appointment to do that. Can you help me fill out the paperwork? There is probably a lot of it."

"Yeah, there probably is. I would be happy to help you with it. We'll work it out together."

"Okay. Thanks."

"What is Tracy going to study? Has he decided?"

"Just general studies to start with. See what he likes to study the most. Sometimes, people go to school for one thing and then find out they don't like it, or it's too competitive. So he doesn't want to commit to something right away."

"That makes sense. He's going to apply to the university?"

"Yeah. I don't know if I want to do U of C or something else. I guess... I have some time to decide. And maybe I'll take a gap year. Work, put away some money, figure out what I want to go into."

Margie hoped Christina would change her mind and want to start her post-secondary education the same year as Tracy. She didn't want Christina to get lost in that gap.

"I'm going to find something for supper and then we can sit down and watch something if you like. Did you finish your homework at Tracy's, or do you need more time?"

"Yeah, I got most of it done. I can do the rest on the bus and before class tomorrow."

"You shouldn't leave it to the last minute."

"I have time in the morning. Why waste it?"

"Well… okay. You're the best judge of how much time it will take. I just worry that if it takes longer than you think, you'll be late handing in the assignment."

"I've got it under control, Mom," Christina told her sternly.

Margie couldn't argue. Christina had been doing well in school despite the challenges. Margie had not received a single call about her missing school, being tardy, or not handing in assignments on time. Her report cards were lower than Margie thought they should be, but this was high school in the big city, and it wasn't going to be as easy for her to get good marks as it had been in a smaller city in junior high. Before all of the COVID disruption.

Margie puttered around the kitchen, pulling together some leftovers, warming them up in the microwave, and virtuously adding a green salad to her plate. She had to watch her weight with all the desk work she did as a detective. It was not as easy as it had been as an active patrol officer. She wasn't putting in as much time running as she had hoped to, either. Getting herself out of bed and onto the multi-use trails nearby was not always easy. Especially in the winter when it was dark, and the trails were frequently icy. It was getting lighter in the mornings now and she should be getting out more.

She sat down to relax and watch whatever Christina had put on the TV.

"How was your day at work?" Christina asked. "You didn't say. Did you have to work on that new murder case?"

"Yes. I talked to the victim's parents and boss and some other people. It is a big case, lots of people involved."

"Why is it so big? I thought it was some guy getting killed in the park. I thought maybe it was homeless guys getting in a fight or something."

"No. It's a lot more complex than that. I can't talk too much about it, but it is…" Margie trailed off, trying to think of how to explain it to Christina in a way that helped her to see how important it was for them to solve the case, without scaring her with talk of possible terrorism.

"It was a computer guy, and it was tied into some other crimes. We're still trying to figure it all out."

"Oh. Some kind of dark web thing? Or one of those ransomware attacks? They are happening all the time now. I don't understand why these big companies and institutions don't have better internet security."

"Yes, you're right. It seems like the bigger they are, the better their security should be. But it seems like the bigger they are, the more holes there are in their network."

Christina nodded. The commercial on the TV ended and her program came back on. Margie nibbled at her salad. Stella lay down on her feet and sighed, happy to have her people home.

CHAPTER SEVENTEEN

*B*ut it wasn't the relaxing evening that Margie had hoped it would be. She had hoped to put all thoughts of the case to the side and just focus on being with Christina and getting the sleep she needed to tackle the case with fresh eyes in the morning.

There was a knock on the door. They rarely had anyone stop by without warning. The occasional person soliciting for furnace sales or a fundraiser, but even that was rare.

Margie stood up. Stella ran at the door, barking wildly, warning whoever it was to stay away from her house.

"Shh, calm down," Margie told her. "We'll just go see who it is, okay? You don't need to rip anyone apart limb from limb until we know who it is."

She checked through the peephole and saw a man a few years younger than she was, with a slim, athletic build and sandy hair. She unlocked and opened the door.

"Lewis?" she looked at the undercover detective in surprise. "What are you doing here?"

"Sorry to bother you at home, but it was… necessary. Can we talk?"

"Of course, come on in."

Margie stepped back and allowed him in. Lewis offered his hand to Stella, and she calmed down and demanded ear scratches rather than threatening to tear him limb from limb.

Lewis had obviously put in a full day of work too. He was clean-shaven as he had been the last time she saw him, no longer playing his undercover role as a homeless man. But he had a five o'clock shadow, and like everyone on Margie's team, his eyes looked tired and possibly swollen.

Christina looked up, surprised, at their visitor. "Mom? What's up?"

"Just someone from work, Christina. This is Detective Riley."

Christina looked the law enforcement officer over. "I don't remember you talking about a Detective Riley on your team."

"No, he's not on my team. But we've worked on a couple of cases together." Margie motioned for Lewis to take a seat in the easy chair. "What's up? Something to do with this... new case?"

"I guess you know most of the details at this point." He rubbed the whiskers on his chin. "I have some concerns."

Margie glanced over at Christina, unsure what she could say in front of her daughter.

"Christina, honey, do you think you could watch that in your room for a few minutes?"

Christina glared at her. "You're home from work. This is supposed to be our time, not work time."

"I know. I don't think this will take long, but I need to hear what Detective Lewis has heard."

Christina sighed, rolled her eyes, and got to her feet.

"Sorry," Lewis apologized. "I didn't mean to disrupt your family time."

Christina ignored him and flounced out of the room. Lewis shook his head at Margie.

"I really am sorry. I'll try to keep it brief. But I couldn't talk to you at the office."

Margie frowned. "Why not?"

She supposed he was working some other undercover role and had to be somewhere else during the day.

"There have been some concerning developments. Your team is handling the murder. And, of course, you are coordinating with other agencies to sort out the drone thing."

Margie nodded but didn't say anything about what they had discovered. She didn't know whether Lewis was close enough to the investigation to be "read in" on it.

"So what's going on?"

"The organization I have been inserted into… has information they shouldn't."

Margie leaned toward him. "You think they were involved in the murder? Who are you working with?"

"They may be the ones running the drone operation. I don't know for sure yet. But it isn't that… it's that they know things about the police investigation. About *your* investigation."

"What about it?"

"They know who you're talking to. Details of what your team has discovered so far. Things they shouldn't know."

A lead weight settled in Margie's stomach. "You think our department has a leak."

"Yes, that's the only explanation I can think of."

Margie rubbed her head, thinking about it. She trusted the detectives she worked with. But there were others in the department that she didn't know as well. And there were administrative positions filled by civilians with access to sensitive information. And there was OCME and the forensics staff. And, of course, they were coordinating with other agencies on the drone attack. YYC security, the RCMP, NAV Canada, Transport Canada; she didn't know all of the agencies that had been brought into it. It was a lot of people and any of them could have access to sensitive information that should not be passed on to whatever organization Lewis had been embedded within.

"How bad is it?"

"I don't know. They don't tell me everything. I haven't been there for long. But if they are behind the drone operation and have someone within the police department or one of the investigating organizations…"

"We need to set up some walls. Make sure we're not sharing everything. Let the other organizations know that… we have concerns."

"How quiet can you keep it?"

"Well… I'm not in charge. I'll need to talk to Sergeant MacDonald. Tell him there is a problem. What organization are you working in?"

Lewis obviously didn't want to tell her that, but put some serious thought into what he could tell her. "It's… an Eastern European organization."

Margie considered that. Eastern European? She'd dealt with the Russian mob in a previous case and sincerely hoped it wasn't them. It was a difficult situation. They would have to be careful not to give Lewis away, but they also needed whatever information he could provide. If he was working for the organization that had put the drone operation in the air, he was the one who could tell them what it was all about. *Maybe.* If he was just freshly inserted and they weren't telling him anything yet, he might not be able to tell the police very much about what to expect. But they had obviously said *something* in front of him or he wouldn't be in Margie's living room.

"Do you have any idea what they are planning to do with the second drone?" she asked.

Lewis chewed on his lip. He looked around the room, looking distracted, but Margie knew he was trying to figure out the right thing to do. It didn't sound like he had met with his handler to pass on the news of the leak or that the organization he was currently a part of had anything to do with the drone operation.

"I have some thoughts, just by the nature of the organization," Lewis said finally. "Not because anyone has confirmed it. They haven't told me that they are involved at all. But it's obvious from what they've said about the drone on the news that they know what its purpose was and what the investigation has revealed so far."

He stared off into the distance, drumming his fingertips on his knee.

"Are we getting close? Will they scrap the plan if we figure it out?" Margie asked.

"They haven't. And I don't think they will. I don't think the police are close enough to deter them. And I don't think you will get close enough before they put it into action."

Margie shivered with a sudden chill. Spring nights were cold. With the warmer daytime temperatures, she forgot how early in the year it was.

"When are they going to put it into action?"

"I don't know for sure." Lewis shook his head in frustration. "I am not in a position to tell you anything helpful, just to tell you to be careful."

"You said something about the nature of the organization. So what is it? 'Eastern European' does not tell me what kind of an organization it is. Are they smuggling drugs? Terrorism does not come to my mind when you say 'Eastern European,' but I confess I don't understand a lot about world politics. I could be completely wrong."

"Not the kind of terrorists that you are thinking of."

"Does that mean it isn't a bomb? Not explosives? What is the payload?"

"I wouldn't discount explosives. But I don't think that is what this is all about. It is more about *information* and power. I don't know whether they are using the drone to physically transfer a package or to do something else. What have you been able to figure out on your end?"

"Siever and the forensic tech guys are examining the computer embedded in the drone. They will be able to figure it out sooner or later," Margie sounded more confident than she was. "The information was encrypted, so it will take them a while to figure out how to access it. Was Xander part of this organization? Cartier doesn't sound Eastern European. He and his parents were fully westernized. They didn't have accents."

Lewis stood up and paced across the room and back. "I can't stay here much longer. People will be looking for me. I don't want them getting anxious about me."

"How are we supposed to figure it out if you won't give me any information?"

"If you can't hack the electronics, then follow the money," Lewis suggested.

He headed for the door. Stella raised her head, wondering why he was leaving already.

"Lewis," Margie protested, frustrated. He might as well not have come. She couldn't use anything that he had said to formulate a plan. She wasn't any better off knowing that there was a leak somewhere in the department and that there was an Eastern European organization involved.

He looked back at her. "Sorry. I'll be in touch. I really do need to get back before they start looking for me. And I don't want to miss anything. If something goes down while I'm here talking to you…"

Margie nodded. "Okay. You know how to find me."

After Lewis was gone, Margie called MacDonald on his cell and filled him in on the developments. He swore.

"That's just what we need on this case. A leak and some Eastern European crime syndicate. I will send out a 'gag order' text and email to the team. No one is to give any information to anyone outside the group without express permission. That includes any civilians or other teams within the police department. That includes OCME, the crime lab, and the mayor. Stay off your phones. Where possible, limit communications to face-to-face and be aware of any possible eavesdroppers."

"We need a 'cone of silence' like on that old spy show."

"We do," he agreed, his voice unamused. "Hold steady for now, Detective Pat. You can answer any calls or contacts from Detective Riley, but don't give him anything without approval. Just the same as everyone else."

Margie swallowed. "Sure. Of course."

"I'll see you in the morning. Unless you have any more contacts from undercover assets."

Margie said goodbye and terminated the call. After staring at the blank screen of the phone for a few minutes, letting her mind wander over everything that had been said or not said, she went to Christina's room.

"He's gone now if you want to continue watching in the living room."

Christina was lying on her stomach watching her tablet and didn't turn around to look at Margie.

"I'm more comfortable here," she mumbled. "You can watch whatever you want."

"If you want to spend some time together…"

"No. I'm tired, I'm going to go to sleep soon."

"I'm sorry about our time together being interrupted by

Detective Riley. It was—is—a very serious situation, and he needed to talk to me."

Christina turned to look at her. "What do you mean, a serious situation?"

"He is undercover right now, and he needed to let someone know that information has been leaked to... bad actors. We need to... make sure that he is protected and that these guys can't get any more information about our investigation."

"Are *you* in danger?" Christina asked worriedly.

"No, I don't think this puts me in any danger. It's dangerous for Lewis to pass information on to us while he is undercover. And it is bad for our investigation if information is getting into the wrong hands. But a physical danger to me? No."

"What if the bad guys followed him here?"

"He is very careful. He would make sure he wasn't followed."

Christina's brow knitted, and she turned back to watch her iPad. She didn't ask Margie any more questions or say she was afraid.

And in a way, that was even worse.

CHAPTER EIGHTEEN

*F*ollow the money, Lewis had said.

It was the only helpful piece of advice he had given her, so she decided to give it her attention. The only financial transaction associated with the case that she was familiar with was the purchase of the two drones by Xander. He had tracked down two used drones that met his specifications, had driven there to inspect them, e-transferred his payment to Paxton, and then the two of them had loaded the drones onto the truck, and he had driven away with them.

At that point, they didn't know where Xander had taken them. Neighbors hadn't reported seeing them, and there was no indication that he had been modifying them at his home. The drones were in some unknown location until one had been launched from Prairie Winds Park and sent to the airport.

They had subpoenaed Xander's account details from the bank, and he'd had some downloaded statements on his laptop computer, which they had managed to unlock.

They had the date that Paxton had received the payment. But Xander did not have that much money in any of his bank accounts and did not show any such transfer. Margie looked at the next and previous months but knew she wouldn't find it. The transfer had to appear on the date Paxton received it, and it didn't.

She didn't know what was involved in back-tracing the e-transfer to see where it had actually come from. Perhaps Xander had other bank accounts that he kept secure, not accessing them on his laptop. Or an account that his financial advisor or father controlled, keeping the money safe but available when he should need it. She put in a request with the forensics guys to see if they could track down where the money had come from.

She sat down with MacDonald and Siever to review what she had discovered.

"Xander was not the purchaser," she told them. "The money did not come from any of his bank accounts I could find. And from what *our friend* told me, this is being run by some organization, not just by Xander or some mysterious partner."

"Where does that get us?" Siever asked. "Does that help us to figure out who it is or what the Raspberry Pi is programmed to do?"

Margie held up her hands, frustrated. "I don't know. From the start, we haven't been able to figure out what Xander's part in this was. So, we know he was the straw buyer in this transaction. We also know that he was a programmer and working with... I don't know. I assume he was involved with computer algorithms and the modification of the drones. He was there when they were purchased and there when the first drone was launched. Maybe he was meant to be a patsy from the start."

"Except that they didn't do anything to make him look guilty," MacDonald pointed out. "If they wanted us to believe that he was the pilot, then at the very least, the controller should have been left with his body. But it wasn't. We always knew that there was another person involved, because he was killed and he didn't have the controller."

"Okay, maybe not a patsy," Margie amended. "But there has been misdirection. Hiding the actual buyer. The actual pilot. They haven't tried to make it look like it was just his project from the start. Or that it was an accident that the drone was launched in restricted airspace or flown to the airport."

There was a knock on the door, and they all looked toward the window to see who it was. Cruz stood at the door, waiting for their signal.

MacDonald beckoned for Cruz to enter, and he did.

"I just got a phone call," he informed them.

"Close the door, please."

Cruz did so, and looked around at them, unsure whether to proceed. MacDonald looked at each of his detectives, weighing the risks against the rewards. He might kick out Margie and Siever and listen to what Cruz had to say, compartmentalizing the information until he was sure it could be shared with the entire team.

"Go ahead," MacDonald said eventually, giving Cruz a nod.

"Yes, sir." Cruz took a deep breath. "I just took a call from CSIS[1]."

Margie raised her brows. They didn't usually have much to do with the Canadian Security Intelligence Service. She wasn't aware that they had been brought in on the drone case, but it made sense, especially now that they knew they were dealing with an Eastern European organized crime

---

1. CSIS is not pronounced by speaking each letter (C.S.I.S.) but as SEA-siss

faction. Lewis had said that it was all about information and power, which put it square in CSIS's domain.

"CSIS," MacDonald repeated, caution in his voice. "What did they want?"

"It was an Agent Bligh. She wasn't looking for information. She was selling, not buying."

"Great. What have you learned?"

"She'd had a phone conversation with Xander Cartier the day before the drone's launch."

Everyone was silent, waiting for more information. Margie had a sense of relief as the pieces started to fall into place.

"Cartier initiated the call. He was concerned about the drones and the work he had done on them. He was worried that they would be used in a way detrimental to national security and infrastructure."

"He was a whistleblower," Margie said. "That lines up with everything we've heard about him. He was not a terrorist. He was not radicalized. He saw what they were doing and tried to warn someone. That is why he was killed."

Cruz nodded. "He did not yet know the target. He didn't know where the drone was going to be launched from. He said he hoped to have that information in a day or two, and he would try to reach out to her again."

"But they stopped him," Siever contributed.

"And then... I asked Agent Bligh to repeat herself, because I wanted you to hear the exact words." Cruz tapped the screen of his phone. They heard the CSIS agent's voice.

"He told me, 'If I can't stop it, and it falls into your hands, the serial number is key.'"

Siever bolted from the room.

CHAPTER NINETEEN

*M*argie stared after Siever, her mouth hanging open. The expressions on Cruz's and MacDonald's faces told her they were just as surprised by his abrupt behavior as she was.

"What was that about?" Cruz asked Margie.

"Uh—I'm not sure. He didn't say anything to me."

They went on without him.

"This clears up a lot," MacDonald said. "But it still doesn't answer the question of how Xander ended up working for this cartel. Did he tell CSIS who he was involved with? Who gave him the instructions on how to modify the drone? Was it a job? Was he moonlighting? Or was it like we were speculating on—a friend or someone he met online?"

"If he was moonlighting, that would explain why his parents thought he was working at night and his boss said he wasn't," Margie suggested.

Cruz and MacDonald nodded.

"He didn't tell her the names of the parties," Cruz said, "He was nervous about his role and didn't want to get anyone in trouble until he could see the whole picture."

"Maybe he thought that others might be in the same position he was," Margie suggested. "People who had gotten involved with the project innocently. He didn't want them to get swept up with everyone else."

"Maybe. Or maybe Xander wasn't as innocent as we would like to believe he was." MacDonald's voice held skepticism. "I assume he got paid for this moonlighting. It was probably a pretty good payday for him. He wouldn't want to turn all that money over to the government."

Margie hadn't considered that he would be asked to give up the proceeds he had been paid. "But he was rich. He came from a rich family; his parents had scads of money. He had a nice home and car himself, and a good job that paid well. He didn't have to worry about being unable to pay the mortgage."

"His father's wealth was not necessarily his. And being wealthy never stopped anyone from wanting more. There is always something you can't afford," MacDonald pointed out.

Margie couldn't come up with an argument to that.

"Will Detective Riley be informed about this by CSIS?" she asked. "Were they calling ALERT as well?"

"Let's keep it to ourselves for the moment," MacDonald cautioned, correctly discerning that Margie wanted to phone Lewis about it herself if CSIS hadn't already reached out to his agency. "For the moment, it doesn't make any difference to the direction of our investigation. And too much information has already been leaked to the cartel Lewis is embedded in. We really don't want them to know that Intelligence is onto this. Keep them thinking that we are floundering and not making any progress in unraveling their plan and being able to stop the second drone."

Margie wasn't sure that they *were* any closer to being able to prevent the actual attack by the cartel. They were all dreading the appearance of the second drone, knowing they were not ready for the havoc the organization had planned. This was not just an impulsive teenager flying a drone into restricted airport territory as a prank. They all knew that whoever had modified the drone planned to do some serious damage, one way or another.

MacDonald pushed himself back from his desk, indicating that the conference was over.

"Thank you all for your work on this. Detective Pat, you have a light touch with Siever. Would you see if you can find out what's going on with him?"

Margie nodded. "Sure, of course."

She exited MacDonald's office and headed toward her own desk. Her thoughts were whirling and she wanted to get down all the random things she needed to follow up on before she could forget anything.

She already had forensics following up on the e-transfer that would show who had paid for the drones and, therefore, who had engaged Xander to modify the drone. It had occurred to her when she had said that Xander had a nice car that when he had picked up the drones he had been driving a truck. He didn't own a truck. She could follow up with Paxton and get a description of the truck. If he could describe it clearly enough, they could put out a BOLO for it. They could look for it on the street cam video taken from around the park and see if they could spot it.

Her desk phone rang. Margie glanced at it and saw it was the tip line they had set up for the case. If she didn't answer it, it would automatically rotate to each detective's phone until someone picked it up. She was supposed to be talking to Siever, so she let it go, trusting that one of the others would pick it up.

Siever was at his desk, eyes fixed on his screen, typing furiously.

Margie didn't want to stand over him, demanding to

know what he was doing. That was just the kind of thing that would get Siever's back up, and he would stubbornly refuse to explain what he was doing or why he had run from MacDonald's office like his hair was on fire.

MacDonald had asked her to use a light touch. Margie understood Siever better than most of the detectives. If she approached it carefully, she thought she could pry the information they needed from him without his getting defensive and closed off.

She grabbed an office chair from a nearby desk that was currently unoccupied. She rolled it closer to Siever's desk and sat down. She pushed herself slowly to his side so that she could see his screen. It was filled with code that didn't mean anything to her.

"How is it going?" she asked Siever.

"Good, good. I'll have it worked out in a few minutes…"

Margie tried not to get too excited. She knew how easily a computer job could turn from 'in a few minutes' to hours or days of frustration as the desired results hovered just out of reach.

"The drone serial number meant something to you?" Margie asked. "I thought he just meant that we would be able to track down the original owner and how he had purchased it for them."

Siever shook his head. "No, no. We already did that. We were looking for the encryption key. It never occurred to me that it would be something that simple."

"You were looking for the encryption key," Margie repeated. The words of the CSIS agent echoed in her mind.

the serial number is key

"Not the serial number is key," she said slowly. "The serial number is *the* key."

Siever stopped what he was doing for a second to look at

Margie, a smile on his face. "The serial number was the encryption key."

"So it allowed you to unlock the files on the Blueberry Pie?"

His lips formed the words to scold her, and then he saw that she was teasing her.

"Raspberry Pi," Margie corrected herself.

"The Raspberry Pi," he agreed.

"And that's what you're looking at? What is it?"

"I have to work it out," Siever said, studying the words on the screen. "It is decrypted, but I still need to figure out what these different routines are doing."

"This looks like it is still encrypted," Margie said, pointing to a line of code. Rather than being commands and variables she could read, there was a string of Cyrillic letters and symbols, obviously still encoded somehow.

"They are not encrypted," Siever disagreed. "They are just not in English. They are comments explaining what each section of the program does. But they are Ukrainian, and Bing Translate isn't getting the nuances."

"Ukrainian?"

Why not Ukrainian? Lewis had told her it was an Eastern European organization. She had assumed Russian, but there was no reason it couldn't be one of those other countries.

"Okay, so we need to find someone who can translate Ukrainian for you? Would that help?"

"That would help," Siever admitted. "But I can figure it out on my own. I can still read the code."

"Okay. I'll see if I can find anyone to help you."

Luckily, Alberta had deep Ukrainian roots. And thousands of refugees had been pouring into the country after the invasion of Ukraine by Russia. There was bound to be someone in the building who could translate Ukrainian and assist Siever.

Margie headed back to her desk.

"Who do you know who speaks Ukrainian?" she asked Jones as she passed by her desk and pulled out her own chair.

She didn't realize until she was sitting down that Jones wasn't answering her because she was on the phone with someone. She mouthed, "Oh, sorry," to Jones and reached for her own phone.

Jones held up one finger, stopping Margie and signaling her to wait. Margie waited, silent, listening to Jones's side of the conversation and watching her jot down notes on her scratch pad. Jones eventually hung up the phone. She looked at Margie, her eyes wide.

"One of the plane spotters we talked to said that a black truck just pulled into Prairie Winds Park. There is something in the bed covered with an orange tarp. She is pretty sure she saw that same truck around the back of the park the day of the drone strike."

Margie swallowed. "Do you think it is the same truck?" Her voice was hoarse. "You think this is the second drone?"

"I asked her if she could tell me the license plate of the truck. She has binoculars to watch the planes."

"Could she see it? I'll run it," Margie hovered her fingers over her keyboard. Jones would need to report this new development to MacDonald immediately. It was not something they would be holding back from the other agencies they were working with. They needed to act quickly to stop the launch of the second drone.

"She could see the lettering on the side of the truck." Jones's face was white. "Ferguson Miller Tech."

Margie felt the blood drain from her own face. "The company that Xander worked for. Carey said they weren't working on drones."

Jones nodded. She stood up to go to MacDonald's office. "He lied."

Carey Stepaniak had lied to them.

The very English name of the company had distracted Margie from paying attention to the boss's name. His very Ukrainian last name.

Xander hadn't been moonlighting. He had been working on the drones as part of his day job. Stepaniak had been convincingly shocked when they had told him of Xander's death, but it had all been an act. He had probably pulled the trigger himself.

"We have to get over there," Margie said urgently, following Jones to MacDonald's office to mobilize their forces.

CHAPTER TWENTY

acDonald knew of a detective on another team who spoke Ukrainian and made the call to have him join Siever. If the second drone was being launched, Siever had only minutes to sort out the code and tell them what they were dealing with.

The rest of the team at the office jumped into their cars and headed to the park. The call went out for any patrol officers in the area to get there, start getting people out of the park, and isolate Carey Stepaniak if they could. All of the other agencies were being called and would get into position at the park, the airport, or other critical infrastructure nearby. Just because he had aimed the drone at the airport the first time, that didn't mean it was the target of the second drone. Stepaniak might have a completely different target for the actual attack.

Margie rode with Jones, but they didn't go to the big public entrance near the wading pool. They went to the back corner they had speculated the first drone had been launched from. Margie saw the black Ferguson Miller truck as they pulled up.

They were the first ones to approach Stepaniak directly. Until then, the priority had been getting the public park users out of harm's way. They didn't want another fatality, and they knew that Stepaniak would not hesitate to shoot someone if he thought it necessary to complete his mission.

And this wasn't just a crank on a mission to cause chaos. This was a carefully planned and executed operation. They were lucky one of the plane spotters had seen Stepaniak. The cops who had been making regular stops at the park to check for trouble had missed him.

Margie was the one who had previously met with Stepaniak, so she took the lead. She climbed out of the car, straightened her clothes, and touched her gun in its holster. Stepaniak was bent over the large black drone on a fluorescent orange launchpad. He looked up when the car pulled in beside his truck and proceeded to tinker with the drone without acknowledging their presence.

"Mr. Stepaniak," Margie used a loud, commanding voice. "Step back from the drone, please."

He obeyed, backing away from it so that he was on the opposite side of the launchpad from them.

Margie's relief at his compliance quickly turned to anxiety as he pulled a controller out of the pocket of his hoodie and began twiddling the joysticks.

"No! Drop the controller!" Margie ordered, drawing her weapon and taking aim. "Sir, I'm not going to ask you twice!"

His eyes on the drone, Stepaniak ignored her and launched the drone. The rotors spun, and with a purr, it lifted off the ground. Margie didn't hesitate, but aimed her gun at the drone and fired off several shots in rapid succession.

The drone moved quickly, faster than she had expected, and her shots had no effect on it. She aimed for the center of the drone, hoping to strike some vital mechanism, but the bullet pinged off and the bird did not slow.

Jones took the opposite approach and, rather than firing at the airborne drone, ran straight at Stepaniak. Margie registered Jones's tackle peripherally but stayed focused on shooting at the drone until it was out of range. She holstered and secured her gun and turned to help Jones.

Jones had Stepaniak on the ground and was cuffing him. She nodded at the controller on the ground. "See if you can bring it back down," she told Margie through gritted teeth.

Margie picked up the controller and started playing with the controls to see their effect. She had only ever flown one drone, a year earlier, but it had not been difficult. The controls were pretty basic. She expected the drone to respond immediately as she moved the joysticks, but it didn't. She tried to direct the drone down, but it was still rising into the sky and started on its westward track toward the airport.

"No!" Margie pushed the controls harder with no effect. "Why won't this work?"

"You're too late," Stepaniak smirked. "The autopilot has engaged. No one can control it now."

Margie stared at the drone as it got farther and farther away. She pulled out her radio.

"The second drone is away," she reported to the rest of the team. They could probably all see it from their varied positions around the park. She could feel everyone's eyes on it as they expected her to bring it down and she could do nothing. "It is running on autopilot. We don't know how to cancel it. Did Siever figure anything out?"

"He's working on it with the Ukrainian translator," MacDonald informed her curtly. He did not censure her for being too late or unable to shoot the drone or bring it down with the controller. She could hear MacDonald giving rapid reports and suggestions to the other agencies on the same radio channel. There were other voices as everyone made suggestions and coordinated their forces.

They had brought down the reconnaissance drone at the airport without a problem. Margie told herself that the same would be true of the second one.

It didn't matter that she hadn't been able to stop it.

They would bring it down by jamming the pilot's signal, just as they had the first one.

Only, this time, the pilot wasn't giving the instructions. The drone was on autopilot. It only followed the preprogrammed instructions on its Raspberry Pi microcomputer.

They could shoot it down. They had known another attack might be imminent. They would have a protocol to follow when the drone reached the airport's perimeter. Flights would be grounded with the news that the second drone was in the air, and everyone would be moved out of range of the drone.

In minutes the drone would be stopped and Stepaniak's plan would fail.

Margie turned to him. "What is the drone's payload? What are its instructions?"

He smiled at her. "You can't do anything to stop it. If they try to shoot it down, they will just set off the explosives." He grinned widely and affected an exaggerated Ukrainian accent. "It will all go boom."

Margie reported on the radio as quickly as possible. "Stepaniak says it is carrying explosives."

"What is its mission?" Jones demanded. "If it is on autopilot, it doesn't hurt anything for you to tell us the plan."

He just continued to smile, sure that the plan would work, and they couldn't do anything to stop it.

"We have already tested the airports' defenses," he pointed out. "We know the protocols they will follow to bring it down. To *try* to bring it down." He laughed. "there is nothing you can do to prevent it."

"What is the point of blowing up anything at the airport?" Margie asked. "This is crazy. Do you really think you'll be able to disrupt air traffic for any length of time? They will just route around whatever damage you cause. They have redundancies. Plans for if something like this happens."

"They haven't planned for this," he assured her. "Trust me, I know."

CHAPTER TWENTY-ONE

*M*argie looked inside the truck, hoping to find something they could use there. Some kind of instructions. A manual. An override code. Something that listed the risks that the operation faced. Anything.

The truck was spotless. There wasn't a scrap of paper in it other than the registration papers in the glove box.

But there was a tablet. Margie turned it on and saw a video feed. She instantly knew that it was the drone's eye view of the airport as it approached. She swore, watching it close the distance to the airport, moving swiftly over a highway she thought was probably Deerfoot Trail. She tapped and swiped the tablet, hoping that controls would appear on the screen that would give the drone directions, abort, or return. Stepaniak had said it was on autopilot and couldn't be controlled with the manual controller, but that didn't mean there was no other way to reach it. Siever had told her that the Raspberry Pi incorporated various wireless protocols. Maybe the drone could be reached with a cellular signal.

But there were no controls on the video feed app to control the drone itself, only to zoom in and out on the video feed. Margie looked for other apps on the tablet that might control it and couldn't find anything. She dialed Siever's number. She knew she probably shouldn't; he was already doing everything he could to break the code and find a way to stop the drone. Calling him was not going to be any help at all. But he answered, putting her on speakerphone and speaking in his curiously flat, unemotional tone.

"Siever here."

"It's Detective Pat. I have Stepaniak's tablet here. I can't see any apps that might control a drone. Is there anything I can look for that might help you?"

She could hear him tapping keys in the background, and murmuring remarks to the woman with him, who Margie assumed was the Ukrainian detective.

"I haven't seen anything in what I have looked at that suggests that the program could be interrupted from a tablet or other outside source once it was started. It is designed with fail-safes to keep it running no matter what. They thought of everything." His voice suggested admiration rather than horror.

"There is a video feed on the drone. I can see its approach on the tablet."

"But you can't control it," he said flatly.

"No," Margie sighed. "It doesn't seem like there is anything I can do."

"They'll have bomb experts at the airport," Siever assured her. "They'll explode it safely."

Margie was slightly reassured by that. She knew that was how the bomb squad operated. They would use a robot to inspect the explosive device, would encase it in a shield, and would explode it safely so that no one would be hurt.

Assuming, of course, that it hadn't been rigged to explode in midair, before even reaching the ground. And if they tried to shoot it out of the air, then, as Stepaniak suggested, they might cause it to explode.

"If I can just get past this section," Siever murmured. "I can't figure out what they are trying to do after delivering the payload. I expected the programmed path to end there, but it keeps going…"

"Maybe it is supposed to return to Prairie Winds Park after the bomb is delivered. So that they can use it again. Or access any reconnaissance that it recorded. Maybe this is just another test of the airport's responses. Maybe there is an escalation each time, and they are also gathering more information so that the next attack can be… worse. Lewis said it is about information and power."

"Okay," Siever said. "If they are trying to gather more information, then what kind of information is it? I thought this routine was to log back in to their servers, but what if…"

Margie stared at the feed from the drone as it approached the ground.

Her heart was in her throat. She could barely breathe, watching the flight from the drone's point of view.

It lowered slowly to the ground. There was a slight rocking motion, and then the drone started to rise again.

"The drone has released its payload," one of the voices on Margie's radio announced. "Bomb squad moving in to isolate and neutralize the device."

Margie breathed a sigh of relief, even though her heart still pounded painfully hard.

The drone's mission had been successful, but it was ineffective.

The bomb squad would destroy the bomb.

"The bomb is a smokescreen," Siever said suddenly, his

voice loud on Margie's phone. "It's a distraction! Detective Riley was right; the target is information. *Data!* Shoot the drone down! Isolate the server. It's there to break into the airport's network."

Margie relayed this information on her radio, speaking loudly to cut through all the voices reporting on the bomb squad's activities.

There was an immediate uproar, with overlapping instructions and responses Margie found impossible to follow. She waited for any more information from Siever to relay to the other agencies, but it was difficult to tell what was happening at the airport.

She held her breath, watching the feed from the drone. She couldn't tell by looking at the video whether it had managed to work its way through some kind of vulnerability in the airport's network security. She thought of all of the organizations that had been reported as having fallen prey to ransomware attacks in the past few months.

It seemed like no organization was immune. There were always holes.

Suddenly, Margie lost the feed on the tablet. It went black. "What happened?" she asked aloud, surprised.

She didn't speak into her radio, which was still a chaos of overlapping voices she didn't want to contribute to. She was blind. There was nothing more she could tell them that would help.

"What?" Siever asked, and she realized he had heard her over the phone.

"The drone's feed went out. I don't know what happened."

Siever sucked in air over his teeth.

Margie waited for it to come back, but it didn't.

"Drone has been neutralized," a voice reported in a

clipped tone. "All parties, report: any other drone launches observed?"

Each agency reported back to the negative, with Margie adding her voice to the others.

"Stand down security alert," the original voice instructed. "RCMP will conduct a final sweep, and flights will resume."

CHAPTER TWENTY-TWO

"What happened?" Jones demanded when they returned to the office for debriefing. "How did they bring the drone down?"

MacDonald flipped through a notepad filled with scribbles to explain the details they hadn't all been able to follow while the crisis was underway.

"They brought the first drone down by jamming the signal from the pilot. That was apparently anticipated, and the drone was able to relay data about the airport's defenses and vulnerabilities back to the cartel so that they could adjust for them in their second attack. That attack was not piloted and the drone would not accept any outside instructions. Everything was preprogrammed algorithms."

MacDonald looked at Siever to make sure he had gotten these details right. Siever nodded.

"Right, Xander copied the code onto the first drone so that if he could not stop its launch, we would be able to see what the second drone was programmed to do and, hopefully, stop it." He grumbled his next words. "Would have been nice if he'd added some English comments to the code instead of having to work through it line by line or have the comments translated."

They all smiled at his gripe, relieved that he had been able to do what he had.

"It was supposed to get access to the airport's ground-services server through the vulnerabilities they had identified —systems tied to fueling, baggage handling, and gate scheduling—and then install ransomware that would take those operations offline until the ransom was paid. With those systems down, no flight could depart safely, so departures and arrivals would be paralyzed, potentially across the country. Every grounded hour runs about six grand per plane— dozens of planes and you're burning six figures an hour before hotels and missed connections. CSIS says this cartel was part of a larger entity offering RaaS services."

Margie obligingly asked the question everyone else was thinking but didn't want to ask. "RaaS?"

"Ransomware as a service," Siever provided. "It is a big business for some Eastern European syndicates. It can be very profitable, raking in tens of millions of dollars to release a target like YYC, which could disrupt infrastructure across the country. Not to mention the panic and loss of confidence such an event would cause."

"So how did they bring down the second drone if they couldn't talk to it and give it instructions?" Jones asked.

MacDonald continued his explanation. "The military apparently has something called an anti-drone gun. When we found out about the second drone purchase and knew that another, more sophisticated attack was planned, the airport looked into getting one. But surprise, surprise: It isn't something you can get on Prime Next Day Delivery. So they arranged to have one brought in by the military until they could get their own."

"That's cool," Margie said. "How does it work? Why

didn't they use it as soon as the drone showed up instead of waiting?"

"There are some dangers to using it. Apparently, crashing a drone carrying explosives is not a good idea, so they monitored it and waited for it to release its payload. Then they jammed the Wi-Fi signal that the drone was using to attack the network and send data out. Usually that also brings down the drone by disrupting any RF signal from the pilot's controller and the GPS signal."

"But in this case, it wasn't navigating by RF or GPS," Siever said, nodding. "It used image recognition of preprogrammed landmarks for navigation and various algorithms to avoid obstacles and attacks." His voice was full of admiration over their ingenuity.

MacDonald nodded. "So the Wi-Fi jamming stopped the hijack attempt, and the drone was in retreat. We would have lost it without Annette."

Everyone in the room was silent, looking at each other, wondering who Annette was.

MacDonald cracked a smile. "The anti-drone gun deploys a physical net to capture the drone. A net."

Margie laughed. So did everyone else, still giddy with relief.

It seemed only fitting that after all of the high-tech programming the cartel had done, after all of the reconnaissance and careful planning, the drone had been caught like a butterfly in a net.

CHAPTER TWENTY-THREE

*M*argie could count on the fact that Christina would be home on time when they had planned to visit Moushoom, Margie's grandfather, who lived in an assisted living center a few blocks away. They enjoyed the walk in the sunshine, the warm spring air, and Stella's puppyish behavior, walking much of the way in companionable silence.

The nursing home residents always enjoyed it when they brought Stella along, and they spent a few minutes in the busy TV room, allowing the other residents to greet and interact with Stella before going up to Moushoom's room.

He was not drowsy as he often was when they arrived for a visit, nodding off in front of the hypnotizing TV he claimed to hate. Instead, the TV was off, and he watched the door, running his sash through his fingers and counting the knots on the fringe. He brightened when they entered.

"I knew you would come today," he saw warmly. "Come, daughters, and give me a hug."

They both bent down over his wheelchair to give him a hug and a peck on the cheek. Moushoom invited them to sit down, and they drew their chairs close to his for an intimate discussion.

"It looks like a beautiful day out there today," Moushoom said, looking out the window.

"It is," Margie agreed. "Hopefully, it will be even nicer next week, and we will all go out for a walk together. This week, they said you need a little more time for your chest to clear."

"I am as healthy as a horse," Moushoom declared, thumping his chest, which made him cough. His cheeks got pink, either with embarrassment or the strain of the cough.

"One more week," Margie told him. "You need to take care of yourself."

He nodded and did not argue further. Christina offered Moushoom a sip of his water. He cleared his throat and patted Christina on the knee. "Tell me about school," he told her. "And about your work," he told Margie.

Margie listened carefully as Christina talked about school, telling him far more about what happened on a day-to-day basis than she ever told Margie. She was grateful for the opportunity to listen without trying to pull more details out of her daughter.

Then Margie talked about the investigation into the drones, only touching on Xander Cartier's death, focusing instead on the drones and how they had been brought down.

"I used to weave nets," Moushoom offered, his old fingers going through the familiar movements so that Margie could almost see the string he used to weave into strong nets. "Usually, we used them for fishing, but you can use them for birds too, if you are very careful and quiet." He mimed throwing a net over his prey. "No bird shot in the flesh. Much easier on the teeth." He tapped one of his front teeth, making Margie and Christina laugh. "It could be very efficient, if you were a good hunter."

"I didn't know you could catch birds with a net," Christina contributed.

"Yes, you can. With practice."

"Was that your favorite kind of hunting?"

"Oh, no," Moushoom shook his head, smiling. "I would rather track deer. Lots more meat, hides, and other useful parts. You can live off of a deer for a long time."

"Is hunting them hard?" Christina prompted.

"Yes, it is difficult. You will lose a lot of deer before you get good at it. But once you understand how to track, how each bent blade and impression in the dirt tells its story, you will not go hungry. Even in lean times, you will be able to find prey. Deer, rabbit, fish, birds. Learn to follow the tracks they leave, and you will succeed."

"Do they always leave tracks?" Christina asked. "What if the ground is too hard?"

"Then you must look harder," Moushoom advised.

YOU MUST LOOK HARDER.

Moushoom's words lingered in Margie's thoughts, and with them, Lewis's advice: "Follow the money."

She opened the shared workspace for the Xander Cartier murder and the drone attacks and searched for the back tracing she had requested of the e-transfer payment to Grant Paxton. By the time the information had come back, the second drone had already been captured. Like its predecessor, the drone was taken apart, and the modified parts, especially the Raspberry Pi microcomputer, were examined.

Tracing the purchase of the various parts used to modify the drones had provided enough information to arrest some of the players in the Ukrainian cartel, though Margie was sure that the bosses were probably well out of reach, not allowing themselves to be associated with the day-to-day operations of the organization.

However, it did not appear that the trace on the e-transfer had been followed up on. The cybercrime experts had sent the information back, but Margie couldn't find any sign that it had resulted in any further arrests.

The purchaser was a numbered company. Not unusual. It made the people involved harder to prosecute, but in Alberta, the directors and shareholders all had to be registered and the bank had to follow the anti-money-laundering "Know Your Client" rules. It was getting harder and harder to obscure this information. Margie followed the faint trail left by her prey. A few searches led to a name that sounded vaguely familiar.

Margie searched through the criminal databases without any luck. She turned to an internet search, wondering if she had heard his name on the news.

It did not pop up in any press releases or news shows, but one search result gave Margie a sick feeling in the pit of her stomach.

CHAPTER TWENTY-FOUR

*M*argie hovered in MacDonald's doorway. He looked up and motioned her in with his fingertips.

"Detective Patenaude?"

"Sir, I was doing some follow-up work on the Cartier case."

"All of the evidence points toward Stepaniak and his cybercrime syndicate. Any additional evidence you find should be forwarded to the Crown."

"But this particular piece of evidence... I thought I should come to you first."

"Okay..." MacDonald pointed to the clear spot on his desk. "Show me what you've got."

As she talked, Margie laid down her papers one at a time so he could see how she had developed the lead.

"I noticed that the e-transfer to Mr. Paxton had not been followed up on."

"And you found that the payment traced back to... an offshore company," he guessed.

"Well, an Alberta company to start with. Numbered company."

"Mm-hmm. And it traces back to…"

"An offshore company. And a man named Clarence Melnyk."

MacDonald's brow furrowed. "A Ukrainian name, I assume."

"Yes." Margie laid down the final piece of paper. An online resume. MacDonald picked it up, skimmed it, and swore. He dropped it back onto the stack. "He's one of ours."

"He's a forensic electronics tech."

MacDonald rubbed his forehead, wincing. "One of the techs who was examining the modified parts of the drone."

"And was unable to decrypt the computer files."

"And could probably have read the Ukrainian comments if he had decrypted it."

Margie nodded.

"So we know where the information leak was," MacDonald sighed.

"Yes, sir."

"Well… great job. It's a good thing you went back and looked for this."

"Just… following the trail."

"Just like a—" MacDonald started, then cut himself off.

"Just like my Moushoom taught me," Margie suggested.

MacDonald nodded. "I'll have ALERT send someone over to take him into custody. Unless you wanted to be in on it."

Margie shook her head. She didn't need to look this young man in the eye. She had done her part.

It was time for Margie to go home for a movie marathon with Christina, watching the exploits of a superhero who used advanced technology to foil evil plots against freedom and justice.

PRAIRIE WINDS PARK

*P*rairie Winds Park was opened in 1990, and when the author was raising her son, it was still being built out. When he was little, there was no more there than the huge sledding hill. It was a difficult hike to the top and an exhilarating ride back down to the bottom. The park was also a great place for plane spotting, as there are always aircraft taking off from the airport and flying overhead.

It would be a great place for kite-flying in the summer, if it were not for the airspace restrictions which forbid even the flying of a kite or helium balloons.

The park was completely redeveloped and reopened in 2015 with an expanded spray park, wading pool, and playground. The playground is very unique, with a slide built into the hill, zip line, climbing equipment, and swings which are great for big kids (grown-ups) as well as some smaller, regular-sized play equipment for littles.

IT ALSO OFFERS TENNIS COURTS, a basketball court, cricket pitch, soccer field, baseball diamonds, and skating. There are a number of small gardens—one featuring a Canada flag made of blooms—walking paths, fitness stations, and a number of picnic tables, as well as the gazebo built for the original opening in 1990.

Did you enjoy this book? Reviews and recommendations are vital to making a book successful.

Please leave a review at your favorite book store or review site and share it with your friends.

Don't miss the following bonus material:
Sign up for mailing list to get a free bonus
Read a sneak preview chapter
Other books by P.D. Workman
Learn more about the author

Get the Parks Pat Survival Pack!

Sign up for my newsletter and receive the **exclusive Parks Pat Survival Pack**, packed with bonus materials and extra goodies you won't find anywhere else.

Stay in the loop on new releases, special offers, and insider content—all delivered straight to your inbox.

Sign up today and start your adventure with Parks Pat!

https://pdworkman.com/the-parks-pat-survival-kit-mystery-police-procedural/

Here's what's inside:
- **Out with the Sunset (Book 1, eBook)**

Begin Margie's journey with her first gripping case as a Calgary homicide officer in the Parks Pat Mysteries.

- **Out with the Sunset (Book 1, Audiobook – Computer Narrated)**

Take the mystery on the go—perfect for your commute, workout, or a walk through the park.

- **Bonus Prequel Story: *Flight of the Bluejay***

Discover Margie's *true beginning*. Before she was a sleuth, she was a pregnant teen on the streets—fighting to survive and find her place in the world.

- **Discover Calgary's Treasures – Photo Minibook**

Step into the beauty of Calgary with this exclusive photo album showcasing the first 15 parks that inspired the series.

- **Digital Wallpapers**

Bring the beauty of Calgary's parks to your phone, tablet, or computer with stunning photography.

SNEAK PEEK AT RESERVOIR
OF SECRETS

CHAPTER ONE

*I*t was the perfect day for a picnic in Glenmore Park. Margie was glad it had warmed up and they could get in their first real outing of the year. Moushoom needed a sweater to keep his old body warm, but the rest of them were in shirt sleeves, enjoying the freedom from coats and mittens and other winter gear. Christina's brown face glowed in the sunlight. She looked happy and carefree, as if school and its accompanying stresses were distant memories. A gentle breeze blew over the reservoir and fluttered the bright green leaves of the trees.

It should have been the perfect day, unfolding just as Margie had planned.

It wasn't even like it was a big family get-together. She and Christina wanted to get the extended family together and have a big gathering of the cousins, but they were starting small, with just their little family, and would work on planning something bigger in the summer, getting everyone organized. Like the family at the picnic area next to theirs. Three generations with a vigorous-looking patriarch at their head. Maybe in his seventies, considering the ages of his children, he looked like he could have challenged any of the other adults there or even the grandchildren to a sports challenge. Running, swimming, weightlifting. She didn't know what his sport was, but it was clear that he followed some kind of regimen to keep himself in shape. He appeared to be a wealthy businessman, but his body was not going to seed from sitting in an office chair all day.

"Mom?" Christina prompted.

Margie pulled her gaze away from the larger family group to look into Christina's inquiring eyes. "Uh, sorry. Did you say something? I was distracted."

"When is Detective Riley supposed to be here? He is coming, right?"

Margie's cheeks warmed. She tried to suppress her body's reaction. She wasn't a silly schoolgirl with a crush. She was a grown woman, a professional, a homicide detective, and yes, she liked Lewis, but she didn't know for sure where their relationship was going. She had invited him to the family picnic on a whim, but she was regretting it.

It wasn't like Christina was upset about it. She hadn't complained about an intruder on their family fun. She seemed to like Lewis and didn't show any jealousy at Margie's attention being taken by someone else. But Margie felt vulnerable and was anxious that things would go well.

"He should be here any time," she told Christina casually, checking the time on the face of her phone. She glanced toward the road that wound around to all the parking areas, looking for his car. "As long as nothing came up. Sometimes our plans get derailed by a call."

Christina snorted. "Like I don't know that!"

Margie looked toward her grandfather. "Are you warm enough, Moushoom? Do you want a blanket?"

He looked thin in the wheelchair. He had always been a small man, probably the result of poor nutrition in his childhood. As he aged, he was shrinking still more. She didn't like to see him diminishing in front of her eyes. If only people didn't have to decline as they got older. She wanted him to be there forever, her strong, spry, energetic grandfather. But that man was fading.

"I am fine," Moushoom insisted, giving her a broad smile. "I'm here with my daughters, enjoying the outdoors instead of being cooped up inside, and I don't need another blanket." He smoothed the one she had already laid across his thin legs to keep him toasty. He wasn't moving around like she was, generating heat with her activity.

Moushoom took a deep breath and let it out, smiling. His eyes went over to the family that Margie had been watching earlier. "What a beautiful family. They must be so happy to all be together."

"We are still going to get the cousins together, aren't we, Mom?" Christina asked, even though she knew very well that they hoped to get the extended family together during the summer. Since Margie and Christina had moved to Calgary in the midst of the COVID lockdown, they had been unable to get together for a large gathering. Restrictions had eased by now, and many people had returned to their previous practices, but Margie was still nervous about the risks of a large gathering. COVID was not gone, despite the creation of the vaccines, and it could easily kill an old man like Moushoom. She was terrified any time there was a viral outbreak at his care center.

"Yes, of course," she agreed. "We will get together as many of the Alberta cousins as we can and have a big party."

"Good," Christina pronounced. "It will be a lot bigger than that party." She indicated their picnicking neighbors with her gaze and looked smug. The extended Patenaude family was considerably larger than the one next to them.

They would have to reserve a venue, rather than just hoping to find a free table as they had today.

"It's not how big a family is that matters," Margie pointed out. "It is how close they are. What their relationships are like. They all seem to be getting along pretty well."

But appearances could be deceiving, and it turned out there was a lot more going on at the neighboring family's picnic than Margie imagined.

The smiling faces and warm, cheerful voices were as misleading as the mirrored surface of the reservoir. It looked as smooth as glass, hiding the danger beneath the surface.

CHAPTER TWO

*S*tella started barking wildly, making Margie jump. She automatically patted her leg to call the dog to her and looked around to see what had agitated her. The midsize dog, mostly brown, was focused on something across the green space.

"Come here, Stella. What is it?"

Stella did not look back at her, continuing to bark. But her ears were forward, curious and welcoming, rather than alarmed or aggressive.

Margie thought at first that Stella had seen a squirrel, but then saw the long-legged man walking across the green grass toward them, a friendly smile on his face.

"Oh, here he is," she told Christina, who, of course, could see with her own eyes. Christina rolled her big brown eyes and busied herself with unpacking more food from the cooler.

"It looks like this is the right place," Lewis told Margie with a big smile. "The park is certainly hopping today."

"Yeah, good thing it isn't dead," Christina quipped. "Or Mom would have to get to work."

"Well, Detective Parks Pat is on the scene," Lewis acknowledged, "she wouldn't have to go too far."

"No dead bodies today," Margie declared. "No accidents, no homicides, just people enjoying the warm spring day, each other's company, and the beauty of nature."

Lewis nodded and gave Margie a friendly smile. He didn't shake her hand or hug her, both of them a little awkward and not sure how to handle the relationship. They were not a couple and this was not a date. They were just friends. Detective Lewis Riley had been invited along as an afterthought when Margie had realized that, back from his latest undercover job, he would be spending Victoria Day by himself. Margie didn't think he should be alone. He needed to be surrounded by friends, to be able to relax in a gathering where he didn't have to pretend to be anything other than what he was.

"Can I help you with anything?" Lewis offered, dispelling the awkward moment.

"I think we've got everything under control," Margie said, looking around. "Just waiting for the fire to burn down a bit so we have some good coals and can get the perfect roasted hot dogs."

Lewis looked at the fire, and to his credit, he did not see the need to grab one of the wiener sticks and push the logs around to "fix" her fire. "Looks great. It's about time I had a good cookout. Thank you for inviting me."

"Christina, Moushoom, you remember Detective Riley?" Margie introduced, though, of course, they all knew who the others were. But they had only met a time or two, and Margie thought it was important to repeat names, for her grandfather especially, to make sure they knew each other.

"Welcome to our fire," Moushoom said, and held out one gnarled hand for Lewis.

Lewis took it and shook gently. "Thank you, Sir."

"Sir," Moushoom chuckled. "We've come a long way from what cops used to call an Indian."

Lewis nodded and smiled. "I hope so," he agreed, "Sir."

Moushoom smiled at that and fingered his Métis sash. He had not worn it as a young man, but it was a badge of honor now, and he showed off his heritage proudly every opportunity he got with the colorful woven sash and other traditional clothing.

Reservoir of Secrets, Book #14 of the *Parks Pat Mysteries*
series by P.D. Workman
can be purchased at pdworkman.com or at your favorite
online retailer

ABOUT THE AUTHOR

P.D. Workman is a USA Today Bestselling author and multi-award winner, renowned for her prolific output of over 100 published works that span various genres. With a knack for crafting page-turners, Workman captivates readers with everything from cozy mysteries like the Auntie Clem's Bakery series to gripping young adult and suspense novels.

A prolific reader and writer since childhood, P.D. Workman crafts emotionally powerful stories that don't shy away from hard topics. Her books tackle mental illness, addiction, abuse, and trauma with raw honesty and compassion, giving voice to the often unheard. If you crave authentic, character-driven page-turners that hit deep and stay with you long after the final page, you're in the right place.

With each new release, fans eagerly anticipate another thrilling blend of thought-provoking storytelling and relatable characters that define P.D. Workman's brand as an author of unforgettable page-turners—gripping tales that leave a lasting impact long after the last page is turned.

> P. D. Workman, does not shy from probing the deep psychological scars of childhood trauma, mental illness, and addiction. Also characteristic of this author, these extremely sensitive issues are explored with extensive empathy, described with incredible clarity, and portrayed with profound insight.

——KIM, GOODREADS REVIEWER

Some of Workman's titles have been translated into Spanish, French, Portuguese, German, and Italian.

Workman began writing at an early age and is a prolific reader as well as writer. She is also passionate about teaching and learning, expresses her creativity through art and cooking, and loves exploring the Calgary parks and green spaces where the Parks Pat Mysteries are set. She was a legal assistant for many years and has done extensive charitable work.

Workman was born and raised in Alberta, Canada, and is married with one adult son.

Please visit P.D. Workman at pdworkman.com to see what else she is working on, to join her mailing list, and to link to her social networks.

If you enjoyed this book, please take the time to recommend it to other purchasers with a review or star rating and share it with your friends!

tiktok.com/@pdworkmanauthor

facebook.com/pdworkmanauthor

x.com/pdworkmanauthor

instagram.com/pdworkmanauthor

amazon.com/author/pdworkman

bookbub.com/authors/p-d-workman

goodreads.com/pdworkman

linkedin.com/in/pdworkman

pinterest.com/pdworkmanauthor

youtube.com/pdworkman

Find P.D. Workman's books at

PDWORKMAN.COM

Scan the QR code below

www.ingramcontent.com/pod-product-compliance
Lightning Source LLC
Chambersburg PA
CBHW031605260626
47154CB00020B/1582